IT LOOKS INSIDE YOU. IT LAYS YOU OPEN TO THE GUT... IT COMES EVERY DAY. OR ALMOST EVERY DAY ... IT IS COMING NOW OF EVENINGS. IT COMES EACH TIME JUST A FRACTION LATER. IT WALKS ACROSS THE DAY AND NIGHT. IT KEEPS CHANGING ITS HOUR BUT THE CHANGE IS VERY SMALL ... IT DOES NOT LEAVE ONE BE.

IT'S THE MIND-SIZZLING SECRET
of
SHAKESPEARE'S PLANET

The Brilliant New Novel by
CLIFFORD D. SIMAK

SHAKESPEARE'S PLANET

Clifford D. Simak

A BERKLEY MEDALLION BOOK
published by
BERKLEY PUBLISHING CORPORATION

Robert P. Mills, Ltd.
156 E. 52nd Street
New York, N.Y. 10022

Library of Congress Catalog Card Number: 75-43651
SBN 425-03394-5

BERKLEY MEDALLION BOOKS are published by
Berkley Publishing Corporation
200 Madison Avenue
New York, N.Y. 10016

BERKLEY MEDALLION BOOK ® TM 757,375

Printed in the United States of America

Berkley Medallion Edition, MAY, 1977

1

THERE were three of them, although sometimes there was only one of them. When that came about, less often than it should, the one was not aware there ever had been three, for the one was a strange melding of their personalities. When they became as one, the transformation was something more than a simple addition of the three, as if by this pooling of themselves there had been added a new dimension which made the sum of them greater than the whole. It was only when the three were one, a one unconscious of the three, that the melding of three brains and of three personalities approached the purpose of their being.

They were the Ship and the Ship was them. To become the Ship or to attempt to become the Ship, they had sacrificed their bodies and, perhaps, a great deal of their humanity. Sacrificed, perhaps, their souls as well, although that was something no one, least of all themselves, ever agreed on. This disagreement, it should be noted, stood quite apart from any belief or disbelief that they might have souls.

They were in space, as was the Ship, and this was understandable since they were the Ship. Naked to the loneliness and emptiness of space as the Ship was naked. Naked at once to the concept of space, which is not understood in its entirety, and to the concept of time, which is, in the final accounting, less understandable than space. And naked, too, they finally found, to those attributes of space and time, infinity and eternity; two concepts that stand beyond the capability of any intelligence.

As the centuries went on, they were collectively convinced they would become, in all truth, the Ship and nothing but the Ship, sloughing off all they had ever been before. But they had not reached that point yet. Humanity still persisted; memory still hung on. They still, at times, felt the old identities, perhaps with some of the sharpness dulled, with the pride less bright; because of the nagging doubt that they had been quite as noble in their sacrifices as they, at one time, had been able to convince themselves. For it finally came to them, although not to all of them at once, but one by one, that they had been guilty of semantic shuffling, using the term *sacrifice* to becloud and camouflage their basic selfishness. One by one, it came to them in those tiny intervals when they were truly honest with themselves, that the nagging doubts which hounded them might be more important than the pride.

At other times, old triumphs and regrets came surging out of time long gone and alone, not sharing with the others, each fondled the old triumphs and regrets, obtaining from them a satisfaction they would not admit, even to themselves. On occasion they stood aside from one another and talked to one another. This was a most shameful thing and they knew that it was shameful, delaying the time when they could finally sink their own identities into the one identity that came about through the consolidation of their three identities. In their more honest moments they realized that in doing this they were instinctively shying away from that final loss of personal identity which is the one outstanding terror all sentient life associates with death.

Usually, however, and increasingly as time went on, they were the Ship, and the Ship alone, and in this there was a satisfaction and a pride, and at times a certain holiness. The holiness was a quality that could not be defined in words or delineated in a thought, for it was outside and beyond any sensation or accomplishment that the creature known as man could have conjured up even in the utmost exercise of his not inconsiderable imagination. It was, in a way, a sense of minor brotherhood with both time and space, the sense of being one, strangely identified, with the space-time concept, that hypothetical condition which is the basic pattern of the universe. Under this condition they were kin to the stars and neighbor of the galaxies, while the emptiness and loneliness, although never losing frightfulness, became familiar ground.

In the best of times, when they most nearly came to their final purpose, the Ship faded from their consciousness and they alone, the consolidated one of them alone, moved across and through and over the loneliness and emptiness, no longer naked, but a native of the universe that was now their country.

2

SHAKESPEARE said to Carnivore, "The time is nearly come. Life fades rapidly; I can feel it go. You must be ready. Your fangs must pierce the flesh in that small moment before death. You must not kill me, but eat me even as I die. And you remember, surely, all the rest of it. You do not forget all that I have told you. You must be the surrogate of my own people since none of them is here. As best friend, as only friend, you must not shame me as I depart from life."

Carnivore crouched and shivered. "It is not something that I asked," he said. "It is not something that I would elect to do. It is not my way to kill the old or dying. My prey must be always full of life and strength. But as one life to another, as one intelligence to another, I cannot refuse you. You say it is a holy thing, that I perform a priestly office and this is something from which one must never shrink, although every instinct in me cries out against the eating of a friend."

"I hope," said Shakespeare, "that my flesh be not too tough nor the flavor strong. I hope the ingestion of it does not make you gag."

"I shall not gag," promised Carnivore. "I shall be strong against it. I shall perform most truly. I shall do everything you ask. I shall follow all instructions. You may die in peace and dignity, knowing that your last

4

and truest friend will carry out the offices of death. Although you will permit me the observation that this is the strangest and the most obnoxious ceremony I have ever heard of in a long and misspent life.''

Shakespeare chuckled weakly. ''I will allow you that,'' he said.

3

CARTER HORTON came alive. He was, it seemed, at the bottom of a well. The well was filled with fuzzy darkness and, in sudden fright and anger, he tried to free himself of the fuzz and darkness and climb out of the well. But the darkness wrapped itself about him, and the fuzziness made it difficult to move. After a time he lay quiet. His mind clicked hesitantly as he sought to know where he was and how he might have gotten there, but there was nothing to give him any answers. He had no memories at all. Lying quietly, he was surprised to find that he was comfortable and warm, as if he had been always there, comfortable and warm, and only aware now of the comfort and the warmth.

But through the comfort and the warmth, he felt a frantic urgency and wondered why. It was quite enough, he told himself, to continue as he was, but something in him shouted that it was not enough. He tried again to climb out of the well, to shake off the fuzziness and darkness, and failing, fell back exhausted.

Too weak, he told himself, and why should he be weak?

He tried to shout to attract attention, but his voice would not work. Suddenly he was glad it didn't, for until he was stronger, he told himself, it might be unwise to attract attention. For he did not know where he was or what or who might be lurking near, nor with what intent.

He settled back into the darkness and the fuzziness, confident that it would conceal him from whatever might be there, and was a bit amused to find he felt a slow, seeping anger at being forced thus to huddle against attention.

Slowly the fuzziness and the darkness went away, and he was surprised to find that he was not in any well. Rather, he seemed to be in a small space that he now could see.

Metal walls went up on either side of him and curved, only a foot or so above his head, to form a ceiling. Funny-looking gadgets were retracted into slots in the ceiling just above his head. At the sight of them, memory began seeping back, and carried by that memory was a sense of cold. Thinking about it, he could not recall an actual coldness, although the sense of cold was there. As the memory of the cold reached out to touch him, he felt a surge of apprehension.

Hidden fans were blowing warm air over him, and he then understood the warmth. He was comfortable, he realized, because he was lying on a soft, thick pad placed upon the floor of the cubicle. Cubicle, he thought—even the words, the terminology, were beginning to come back. The funny-looking gadgets stored in the ceiling slots were part of the life-support system, and they were there, he knew, because he didn't need them any more. The reason he didn't need them any more, he realized, was that Ship had landed.

Ship had landed and he had been awakened from his cold-sleep—his body thawed, the recovery drugs shot into his bloodstream, carefully measured doses of high-energy nutrients fed slowly into him, massaged and warmed and alive once more. Alive, if he had been dead. Remembering, he recalled the endless discussions over this very question, mulling over it, chewing it, lacerating it, shredding it to pieces and then trying to put the pieces meticulously back together. They called it cold-sleep, sure—they *would* call it that, for it had a soft and easy sound. But was it sleep or death? Did one go to sleep and wake? Or did one die and come to resurrection?

It didn't really matter now, he thought. Dead or sleeping, he was now alive. I be damned, he told himself, the system really worked—realizing for the first time that he had held some doubt of it really working despite all the experiments that had been carried out with mice and dogs and monkeys. Although, he remembered, he had never spoken of the doubts, concealing them not only from the others, but from himself as well.

And if he were here alive, so would the others be. In just a few more minutes he'd crawl out of the cubicle and the others would be there, the four of them reunited. It seemed only yesterday that they had been together—as if they'd spent the evening in one another's company and now, after a short night's sleep, had awakened from a dreamless night. Although he knew it would be much longer than that—as much as a century, perhaps.

He twisted his head to one side and saw the hatch, with the port of heavy glass set into it. Through the glass he could see into the tiny room, with the four lockers ranged against the wall. There was no one about—which meant, he told himself, the others were still in their cubicles. He considered shouting to them, but thought better of it. It would be unseemly, he thought—too exuberant and somewhat juvenile.

He reached out a hand to the latch and pulled down on it. It operated stiffly, but finally he got it down and the hatch swung out. He jackknifed his legs to thrust them through the hatch and had trouble doing it, for there was little room. But finally he got them through, and twisting his body, slid carefully to the floor. The floor was icy to his feet, and the metal of the cubicle was cold.

Stepping quickly to the adjacent cubicle, he peered through the glass of the hatch and saw that it was empty, with the life-supports retracted into the ceiling slots. The other two cubicles were empty as well. He stood transfixed with horror. The other three, revived, would not have left him. They would have waited for him so they all could go out together. They would have done this, he was convinced, unless something unforeseen had happened. And what could have happened?

Helen would have waited for him, he was sure of that. Mary and Tom might have left, but Helen would have waited.

Fearfully, he lunged at the locker that had his name upon it. He had to jerk hard on the handle once he had turned it to get the locker open. The vacuum inside the locker resisted, and when the door came open, it opened with a pop. Clothing hung upon the racks and footwear was ranged neatly in a row. He grabbed a pair of trousers and climbed into them, forced his feet into a pair of boots. When he opened the door of the suspension room, he saw that the lounge was empty and the ship's main port stood open. He raced across the lounge to the open port.

The ramp ran down to a grassy plain that swept off to the left. To the right, rugged hills sprang up from the plain and beyond the hills a mighty mountain range, deep blue with distance, reared into the sky. The plain was empty except for the grass, which billowed like an ocean as wind gusts swept across it. The hills were covered with trees, the foliage of which was black and red. The air had a sharp, fresh tang to it. There was no one in sight.

He went halfway down the ramp and still no one was in sight. The planet was an emptiness and the emptiness seemed to be reaching out for him. He started to cry out to ask if anyone were there, but fear and the emptiness dried up the words and he could not get them out. He shivered in the realization that something had gone wrong. This was not the way it should be.

Turning, he went clumping up the ramp and through the lock.

"Ship!" he yelled. "Ship, what the hell is going on?"

Ship said, calmly, unconcernedly, inside his mind, *What's the problem, Mr. Horton?*

"What's going on?" yelled Horton, more angry now than frightened, angered by the supercilious calmness of this great monster, Ship. "Where are all the others?"

Mr. Horton, said Ship, *there aren't any others.*

"What do you mean there aren't any others? Back on Earth there was a team of us."

You are the only one, said Ship.

"What happened to the others?"

They are dead, said Ship.

"Dead? How do you mean, dead? They were with me just the other day!"

They were with you, said Ship, *a thousand years ago.*

"You're insane. A thousand years!"

That's the span of time, said Ship, speaking still inside his mind, *we have been gone from Earth.*

Horton heard a sound behind him and spun about. A robot had come through the port.

"I am Nicodemus," said the robot.

He was an ordinary robot, a household service robot, the kind that back on Earth would be a butler or a valet, or a cook or errand boy. There was no mechanical sophistication about him; he was just a sloppy, slat-footed piece of junk.

You need not, said Ship, *be so disdainful of him. You will find him, we are sure, to be quiet efficient.*

"Back on Earth . . ."

Back on Earth, said Ship, *you trained with a mechanical marvel that had far too much that could go wrong with it. Such a contraption could not be sent out on a long-haul expedition. There would be too much chance of it breaking down. But with Nicodemus there is nothing to go wrong. Because of his simplicity he has high survival value.*

"I am sorry," Nicodemus said to Horton, "that I was not present when you woke. I had gone out for a quick scout around. I had thought there was plenty of time to get back to you. Apparently, the recovery and reorientation drugs worked much more swiftly than I'd thought. It usually takes a fair amount of time for recovery from cold-sleep. Especially cold-sleep of such long duration. How are you feeling now?"

"Confused," said Horton. "Completely confused. Ship tells me I am the only human left, implying that the others died. And he said something about a thousand years . . ."

To be exact, said Ship, *nine hundred fifty-four years, eight months and nineteen days.*

"This planet," said Nicodemus, "is a very lovely one. In many ways like Earth. Slightly more oxygen, a bit less gravity . . ."

"All right," said Horton, sharply, "after all these years we are finally landed on a very lovely planet. What happened to all the other lovely planets? In almost a thousand years, moving close to the speed of light, there must have been . . ."

"Very many planets," Nicodemus said, "but none of them lovely. Nothing a human could exist upon. Young planets, with the crusts unformed, with fields of bubbling magma and great volcanoes, vast pools of molten lava, the sky seething with boiling clouds of dust and poisonous vapors and as yet no water and little oxygen. Old planets slipping down to death, the oceans dry, the atmosphere thinned out, without sign of life upon them—life, if it ever had existed, now wiped out. Massive gas planets rolling along their orbits like great striped marbles. Planets too close to their suns, scoured by solar radiation. Planets too far from their suns, with glaciers of frozen oxygen, seas of slushy hydrogen. Other planets that somehow had gone wrong, clothed in atmosphere deadly to all life. And a few, a very few, too lusty with life—jungle planets occupied by ravening life-forms so hungry and ferocious that it would have been suicidal to set foot upon them. Desert planets where life had never started—barren rock, with no soil ever formed, with very little water, the oxygen locked in eroding rock. We orbited some of the planets that we found; we merely glanced at others. A few we landed on. Ship has all the data if you want a printout."

"But now we've found one planet. What do we do now—look it over and go back?"

No, said Ship, *we can't go back.*

"But this is what we came out for. We and the other ships, all of them hunting planets the human race could colonize."

We've been out too long, said Ship. *We simply can't*

go back. We've been out almost a thousand years. If we started back right now, it would take almost another thousand years. Perhaps a little less, for we'd not be slowing down to have a look at planets, but still not too far from two thousand years from the time we left. Perhaps a great deal longer, for time dilation would be a factor, and we have no reliable data on dilation. By now we've probably been forgotten. There would have been records, but more likely they now are lost or forgotten or misplaced. By the time we got back, we'd be so outdated that the human race would have no use for us. We and you and Nicodemus. We'd be an embarrassment to them, reminding them of their bumbling attempts of centuries before. Nicodemus and we would be technologically obsolescent. You'd be obsolescent as well, but in another way—a barbarian come from the past to haunt them. You'd be outdated socially, ethically, politically. You'd be, by their standards, a possibly vicious moron.

"Look," protested Horton, "there is no sense in what you say. There were other ships . . ."

Perhaps some of them found suitable planets, said Ship, shortly after they had left. In such cases they could safely have returned to Earth.

"But you went on and on."

Ship said, We performed our mandate.

"You mean, you hunted planets."

We hunted for one particular planet. The kind of planet where man could live.

"And took almost a thousand years to find it."

There was no limit on the search, said Ship.

"I suppose not," said Horton, "although it was something we never thought about. There were a lot of things we never thought about. A lot of things, I suppose, we were never told. Then tell me this: Suppose you'd not found this planet. What would you have done?''

We'd have kept on searching.

"A million years, perhaps?''

If need be, a million years, said Ship.

"And now, having found it, we cannot go back.''

That is correct, said Ship.

"So what's the good of finding it?'' asked Horton. "We find it, and Earth will never know we found it. The truth of the matter is, I think, that you have no interest in returning. There is nothing back there for you.''

Ship made no answer.

"Tell me,'' Horton cried. "Admit it.''

Nicodemus said, "You'll get no answer now. Ship stands on silent dignity. You have offended it.''

"To hell with Ship,'' said Horton. "I've heard enough from them. I want some answers from you. Ship said the other three are dead . . .''

"There was a malfunction,'' said Nicodemus. "About a hundred years out. One of the pumps ceased functioning, and the cubicles heated up. I managed to save you.''

"Why me? Why not one of the others?''

"It was very simple,'' said Nicodemus, reasonably. "You were number one in line. You were in cubicle number one.''

"If I had been in cubicle number two, you would have let me die.''

"I let no one die. I was able to save one sleeper. Having done that, it was too late for the others.''

"You did it by the numbers?''

"Yes,'' said Nicodemus, "I did it by the numbers. Is there a better way?''

"No,'' said Horton. "No, I guess there's not. But

when three of us were dead, was there no thought of aborting the mission and going back to Earth?''

''There was no thought of it.''

''Who made the decision? I imagine Ship.''

''There was no decision. Neither of us ever mentioned it.''

It had all gone wrong, thought Horton. If someone had sat down and worked at it, with wholehearted concentration and a devotion that fringed on fanaticism, they couldn't have done a better job of screwing it all up.

A ship, one man, one flat-footed stupid robot— Christ, what an expedition! And, furthermore, a pointless one-way expedition. We might just as well not have started out, he thought. Except that if they hadn't started out, he reminded himself, he'd now be dead for many centuries.

He tried to remember the others, but could not remember them. He could see them only dimly, as if he were seeing them through fog. They were indistinct and blurred. He tried to make out their faces and they seemed to have no faces. Later on, he knew, he'd mourn them, but he could not mourn them now. There was not enough of them to mourn. There was no time now for mourning them; there was too much to do and to think about. A thousand years, he thought, and we won't be going back. For Ship was the only one that could take them back, and if Ship said it wasn't going back, that was the end of it.

''The other three?'' he asked. ''Burial in space?''

''No,'' said Nicodemus. ''We found a planet where they'll rest through all eternity. Do you want to know?''

''If you please,'' said Horton.

4

FROM the platform of the high plateau where Ship had landed, the planetary surface stretched out to distant, sharp horizons, a land with great blue glaciers of frozen hydrogen creeping down the slopes of black and barren rock. The planet's sun was so distant that it seemed only a slightly larger, brighter star—a star so dimmed by distance and by dying that it did not have a name or number. On the charts of Earth there was not even a pinprick marking its location. Its feeble light never had been registered on a photographic plate by a terrestrial telescope.

Ship, asked Nicodemus, *is this all that we can do?*

Ship said, *We can do no further.*

It seems cruel to leave them here, in this place of desolation.

We sought a place of solitude for them, said Ship, *a place of dignity and aloneness, where nothing will find them and disturb them for study or display. We owe them this much, robot, but when this is done, it is all that we can give them.*

Nicodemus stood beside the triple casket, trying to fix the place forever in his mind, although, as he looked out across the planet, he realized there was little he could fix. There was a deadly sameness here; wherever one might look at it all seemed to look the same. Perhaps, he thought, it is just as well—they can lie here in their anonymity, masked by the unknownness of their final resting place.

There was no sky. Where there should have been a sky was only the black nakedness of space, lighted by a heavy sprinkle of unfamiliar stars. When he and Ship were gone, he thought, for millennia these steely and unblinking stars would be eyes staring down at the three who lay within the casket—not guarding them, but watching them—staring with the frosty glare of ancient, moldering aristocrats regarding, with frigid disapproval, intruders from beyond the pale of their social circle. But the disapproval would not matter, Nicodemus told himself, for there now was nothing that could harm them. They were beyond all harm or help.

He should say a prayer for them, he thought, although he'd never said a prayer before nor ever thought of praying. He suspected, however, that prayer by such as he might not be acceptable, either to the humans lying there or whatever deity might bend his ear to hear it. But it was a gesture—a slender and uncertain hope that somewhere there might still be an agency of intercession.

And if he did pray, what could he say? Lord, we leave these creatures in your care—

And once he had said that? Once he had made a good beginning?

You might lecture him, said Ship. *You might impress upon him the importance of these creatures with whom you are concerned. Or you might plead and argue for them, who need no pleading and are beyond all argument.*

You mock me, said Nicodemus.

We do not mock, said Ship. *We are beyond all mockery.*

I should say some words, said Nicodemus. *They would expect it of me. Earth would expect it of me. You were human once. I would think there'd be, on an occasion such as this, some humanity in you.*

We grieve, said Ship. *We weep. We feel a sadness in us. But we grieve at death, not at the leaving of the dead in such a place. It matters not to them wherever we may leave them.*

Something should be said, Nicodemus insisted to himself. Something solemnly formal, some intonation of studied ritual, all spoken well and properly, for they'll be here forever, the dust of Earth transplanted. Despite all our logic in seeking out a loneliness for them, we should not leave them here. We should have sought a green and pleasant planet.

There are, said Ship, *no green and pleasant planets.*

Since I can find no proper words to say, said the robot to the Ship, *do you mind if I stay awhile? We should at least do them the courtesy of not hurrying away.*

Stay, said Ship. *We have all eternity.*

"And do you know," Nicodemus said to Horton, "I never did get around to saying anything."

Ship spoke. *We have a visitor. He came out of the hills and is waiting just beyond the ramp. You should go out to meet him. But be alert and cautious and strap on your sidearms. He appears an ugly customer.*

5

THE visitor had halted some twenty feet beyond the end of the ramp and was waiting for them when Horton and Nicodemus came out to meet him. He was human-tall and stood upon two legs. His arms, hanging limply at his side, did not end in hands, but in a nest of tentacles. He wore no clothing. His body was covered by a skimpy, molting coat of fur. That he was a male was aggressively apparent. His head appeared to be a bare skull. It was innocent of hair or fur, and the skin was tightly stretched over the structure of the bones. The jaws were heavy and elongated into a massive snout. Stabbing teeth, set in the upper jaw, protruded downward, somewhat like the fangs of the primitive saber-tooth of ancient Earth. Long, pointed ears, pasted against the skull, stood rigid, overtopping the bald, domed cranium. Each of the ears was tipped with a bright red tassle.

As they reached the bottom of the ramp, the creature spoke to them in a booming voice. "I welcome you," he said, "to this asshole of a planet."

"How the hell," blurted Horton, startled, "do you know our language?"

"I learned it all from Shakespeare," said the creature. "Shakespeare taught it to me. But Shakespeare now is dead, and I miss him greatly. I am desolate without him."

"But Shakespeare is a very ancient man and I do not understand . . ."

"Not an ancient one at all," the creature said, "although not really young, and he had a sickness in him. He described himself as human. He looked very much like you. I take it you are human, too, but the other is not human, although it has human aspects."

"You are right," said Nicodemus. "I am not a human. I am the next best thing to human. I am a human's friend."

"Then that is fine," said the creature, happily. "That is fine indeed. For I was that to Shakespeare. The best friend he ever had, he said. I surely miss the Shakespeare. I admire him very greatly. He could do many things. One thing he could not do was to learn my language. So perforce I must learn his. He told me about great carriers that go noisily through space. So when I hear you coming, I hurry very fast, hoping that it be some of Shakespeare's people coming."

Horton said to Nicodemus. "There is something very wrong here. Man could not be this far out in space. Ship fooled around, of course, slowing down for planets and it took a lot of time. But we're close to a thousand light-years out . . ."

"Earth by now," said Nicodemus, "may have faster ships, going many times the speed of light. Many of such ships may have overleaped us as we crawled along. So, peculiar as it may seem . . ."

"You talk of ships," the creature said. "Shakespeare talk of them as well but he need no ship. Shakespeare come by tunnel."

"Now, look here," said Horton, a trifle exasperated, "try to talk some sense. What is this tunnel business?"

"You mean you do not know of tunnel that runs among the stars?"

"I've never heard of it," said Horton.

"Let's back up," said Nicodemus, "and try to get another start. I take it you are a native of this planet."

"Native?"

"Yes, native. You belong here. This is your home planet. You were born here."

"Never," said the creature, most emphatically. "I would not urinate upon this planet could I avoid it. I would not stay a small time-unit could I get away. I came hurriedly to bargain outward passage with you when you leave."

"You came as Shakespeare did? By tunnel?"

"Of course, by tunnel. How otherwise I get here?"

"Then leaving should be simple. Go to the tunnel and depart by it."

"I cannot," the creature wailed. "The damn tunnel does not work. It has gone haywire. It works only one way. It brings you here, but does not take you back."

"But you said a tunnel to the stars. I gained the impression it goes to many stars."

"To more than the mind can count, but here it need repair. Shakespeare try and I try, but we cannot fix it. Shakespeare pound upon it with his fists, he kick it with his feet, he yell at it, calling terrible names. Still it does not work."

"If you are not of this planet," said Horton, "perhaps you'll tell us what you are."

"That is simply said. I am a carnivore. You know carnivore?"

"Yes. The eater of other forms of life."

"I am a carnivore," the creature said, "and satisfied to be one. Proud of being one. There be among the stars those who look with disdain and horror upon carnivore. They say, mistakenly, it is not right to eat one's fellow beings. They say it be cruel to do so, but I tell you there is no cruelty. Quick death. Clean death. No suffering at all. Better than sickness and old age."

"All right, then" said Nicodemus. "No need to carry on. We hold nothing against a carnivore."

"Shakespeare say humans also carnivores. But not as much as me. Shakespeare shared the meat I killed. Would have killed himself, but not as good as me. I glad to kill for Shakespeare."

"I bet you were," said Horton.

"You are alone here?" asked Nicodemus. "You are the only one of your kind upon the planet?"

"The only one," said Carnivore. "I arrive on sneaky trip. I tell no one of it."

"This Shakespeare of yours," said Horton. "He was on a sneaky trip as well?"

"There were unprincipled creatures who would have liked to find him, claiming he had done them imaginary harm. He had no wish for them to find him."

"But Shakespeare now is dead?"

"Oh, he's dead, all right. I ate him."

"You what?"

"The flesh only," said Carnivore. "Careful not to eat the bones. And I don't mind telling you he was tough and stringy and not of a flavor that I relished. He had a strange taste to him."

Nicodemus spoke hastily to change the subject. "We would be glad," he said, "to come to the tunnel with you and see about the fixing of it."

"Would you, in all friendship, do that?" Carnivore

asked gratefully. "I was hoping that you would. You can fix the goddamn tunnel?"

"I don't know," said Horton. "We can have a look at it. I'm not an engineer . . ."

"I," said Nicodemus, "can become an engineer."

"The hell you can," said Horton.

"We will have a look at it," said this madman of a robot.

"Then it is all settled?"

"You can count on it," said Nicodemus.

"That is good," said Carnivore. "I show you ancient city and . . ."

"There is an ancient city?"

"I speak too hugely," said Carnivore. "I let my enthusiasm at the fixing of the tunnel to run off with me. Perhaps not an actual city. Perhaps an outpost only. Very old and very ruined, but interesting, perhaps. But now I must be going. The star is riding low. Best to be undercover when darkness is come upon this place. I am glad to meet you. Glad Shakespeare's people come. Hail and farewell! I see you in the morning and the tunnel fixed."

He turned abruptly and trotted swiftly into the hills, without pausing to look back.

Nicodemus shook his head. "There are many mysteries here," he said. "Much to ponder on. Many questions to be asked. But first I must get dinner for you. You've been out of cold-sleep long enough for it to be safe to eat. Good, substantial food, but not too much at first. You must curb your greediness. You must take it slow."

"Now just a goddamn minute," Horton said. "You have some explaining to be done. Why did you head me off when you knew I wanted to ask about the eating of this Shakespeare, whoever he might be? What do you mean, you can become an engineer? You know damn well you can't.''

''All in good time,'' said Nicodemus. ''There is, as you say, explaining to be done. But first you must eat, and the sun is almost set. You heard what the creature said about being undercover when the sun is gone.''

Horton snorted. ''Superstition. Old wives' tales.''

''Old wives' tales or not,'' said Nicodemus, ''it is best to be ruled by local custom until one is sure.''

Looking out across the sea of billowing grass, Horton saw that the level horizon had bisected the sun. The sweep of grass seemed to be a sheet of shimmering gold. As he watched, the sun sank deeper into the golden shimmer and as it sank, the western sky changed to a sickly lemon-yellow.

''Strange light effect,'' he said.

''Come on, let's get back aboard,'' urged Nicodemus. ''What do you want to eat? Vichyssoise, perhaps—how does that sound to you? Prime ribs, a baked potato?''

''You set a good table,'' Horton told him.

''I am an accomplished chef,'' the robot said.

''Is there anything you aren't? Engineer and cook. What else?''

''Oh, many things,'' said Nicodemus. ''I can do many things.''

The sun was gone and a purple haze seemed to be sifting down out of the sky. The haze hung over the yellow of the grass, which now had changed to the color of old, polished brass. The horizon was jet-black except for a glow of greenish light, the color of young leaves, where the sun had set.

''It is,'' said Nicodemus, watching, ''most pleasing to the eye.''

The color was fading rapidly, and as it faded, a chill crept across the land. Horton turned to go up the ramp. As he turned, something swooped down upon him, seizing him and holding him. Not really seizing him, for there was nothing there to seize him, but a force that fastened on him and engulfed him so he could not move. He tried to fight against it, but he could not move a muscle. He attempted to cry out, but his throat and tongue were frozen. Suddenly he was naked—or felt that he was naked, not so much deprived of clothes as of all defenses, laid open so that the deepest corner of his being was exposed for all to see. There was a sense of being watched, of being examined, probed, and analyzed. Stripped and flayed and laid open so that the watcher could dig down to his last desire and his final hope. It was, said a fleeting thought inside his mind, as if God had come and was assessing him, perhaps passing judgment on him.

He wanted to run and hide, to jerk the flayed skin back around his body and to hold it there, covering the gaping, spread-eagled thing that he had become, hiding himself again behind the tattered shreds of his humanity. But he couldn't run and there was no place to hide, so he continued, standing rigid, being watched.

There was nothing there. Nothing had appeared. But something had seized and held and stripped him, and he tried to drive out his mind to see it, to learn what kind of thing it was. And as he tried to do this, it seemed his skull cracked open and his mind was freed, protruding and opening out so that it could encompass what no man had ever understood before. In a moment of blind panic, his mind seemed to expand to fill the universe, clutching with nimble mental fingers at everything within the confines of frozen space and flowing time and for an instant, but only an instant, he imagined that he saw deep into the core of the ultimate meaning hidden in the farthest reaches of the universe.

Then his mind collapsed and his skull snapped back together, the thing let loose of him and, staggering, he reached out to grasp the railing of the ramp to hold himself erect.

Nicodemus was beside him, supporting him, and his anxious voice asked, "What is the matter, Carter? What came over you?"

Horton grasped the railing in a death grip, as if it were the one reality left to him. His body ached with tension, but his mind still retained some of its unnatural sharpness, although he could feel the sharpness fading. Helped by Nicodemus, he straightened. He shook his head and blinked his eyes, clearing his vision. The colors out on the sea of grass had changed. The purple haze had faded into a deep twilight. The brassiness of the grass had smoothed into a leaden hue, and the sky was black. As he watched, the first bright star came out.

"What is the matter, Carter?" the robot asked again.

"You mean you didn't feel it?"

"Something," said Nicodemus. "Something frightening. It struck me and slid off. Not my body, but my mind. As if someone had used a mental fist and had missed the blow, merely brushing against my mind."

6

THE brain-that-once-had-been-a-monk was frightened, and the fright brought honesty. Confessional honesty, he thought, although never in the confessional had he ever been as honest as he was being now.

What was that? asked the grande dame. *What was that we felt?*

It was the hand of God, he told her, *brushed against our brow.*

That's ridiculous, said the scientist. *I note it; that is all. A manifestation of some sort. From far out in space, perhaps. Not a product of this planet. I have the distinct impression that it was not of local origin. But until we have more data, we must make no attempt to characterize it.*

That's the sheerest twaddle I have ever heard, said the grande dame. *Our colleague, the priest, did better.*

Not a priest, said the monk. *I have told you. A monk. A mere monk. A very piss-poor monk.*

And that was what he'd been, he told himself, continuing with his honest self-assessment. He never had been more. A less-than-nothing monk who had been afraid of death. Not the holy man that he had been acclaimed, but a sniveling, shivering coward who was afraid to die, and no man who was afraid of death ever could be holy. To the truly holy, death must be a promise of a new beginning and, thinking back, he knew he never had been able to conceive of it as anything but an end and nothingness.

For the first time, thinking thus, he was able to admit what he never had been able to admit before, or honest enough to admit before—that he had seized the opportunity to become the servant of science to escape the fear of death. Although he knew he had purchased only a deferment of his death, for even as the Ship, he could not escape it altogether. Or at least could not be certain he'd escape it altogether, for there was the chance—the very slightest chance—which the scientist and the grande dame had discussed centuries ago, with himself staying strictly out of the discussion, afraid to enter it, that as the millennia went on, if they survived that long, the three of them possibly could become pure mind alone. And if that should prove to be the case, he thought, then they could become, in the strictest sense, immortal and eternal. But if this did not happen, they still must face the fact of death, for the spaceship could not last forever. In time it would become, for one reason or another, a shattered, worn-out hulk adrift between the stars, and in time no more than dust in the cosmic wind. But that would not be for a long time yet, he told himself, grasping at the hope. The Ship, with any luck, might survive millions of years, and that might give the three of them the time they needed to become pure mind alone—if, in fact, it was possible to become pure mind alone.

Why this overriding fear of death, he asked himself. *Why this cringing from it, not as an ordinary man would cringe, but as someone who was obsessed with a repugnance against the very thought of it? Was it, perhaps, because he'd lost his faith in God, or perhaps, which was even worse, had never achieved a faith in*

God? And if that were the case, why had he become a monk?

Having got a start with honesty, he gave himself an honest answer. He had chosen monking as an occupation (not a calling, but an occupation) because he feared not only death, but even life itself, thinking that it might be easy work which would provide him shelter against the world he feared.

In one thing, however, he had been mistaken. Monking had not proved an easy life, but by the time he'd found this out, he was afraid again—afraid of admitting his mistake, afraid of confessing, even to himself, the lie that he was living. So he had gone on as a monk and in the course of time, in one way and another (more than likely by pure happenstance) had achieved a reputation for a piety and devotion that was at once the envy and the pride of all his fellow monks, although some of them, on occasion, delivered some rather unworthy snide remarks. As time went on, it seemed that somehow a great many people came to hear of him—not perhaps for anything he had ever done (for, truth to tell, he had done but little), but for the things he seemed to stand for, for his way of life. As he thought about it now, he wondered whether there had not been a misconception—if his piety may not have stemmed from his devotion, as everyone seemed to think, but from his very fear and, because of his fear, his conscious attempts at self-effacement. A trembling mouse, he thought, that became a holy mouse because of its very trembling.

But however that might have been, he finally came to stand as a symbol for the Age of Faith in a materialistic world and one writer who had interviewed him described him as a medieval man persisting into modern times. The profile that came from the interview, published in a magazine of wide circulation and written by a perceptive man who, for dramatic effect, did not hesitate to gild the lily slightly, had provided the impetus that, after several years, had elevated him to greatness as a simple man who held the necessary insight to return to basic faith and the strength of soul to hold that faith against the inroads of humanistic thought.

He could have been an abbot, he thought with a surge of pride; perhaps more than an abbot. And when he became aware of the pride, made no more than a token effort to quash it. For pride, he thought, pride and, finally, honesty, were all that he had left. When the abbot had been called to God, it had been made known to him in various subtle ways, that he could succeed the abbot. But, suddenly afraid again, this time of responsibility and place, he had pleaded to remain with his simple cell and simple tasks, and because the order held him in high regard, he was granted his petition. Although, thinking of it since and now drenched in honesty, he allowed the suspicion that he had suppressed before out into the open. It was this: had his petition been granted not because of the order's high regard of him, but because the order, knowing him too well, had realized what a poor stick of an abbot he would have made? In view of the favorable publicity his appointment would have afforded because of the wide acclaim which had been accorded him, had the order been forced into a position where it had felt bound to make at least the offer? And had there been a wholehearted sigh of relief throughout the entire house when he had declined?

Fear, he thought—a man hounded all his life by fear—if not a fear of death, then the fear of life itself. Maybe, after all, there had been no need of fear. Perhaps, after all the fearfulness, there had been nothing actually to fear. It had been, more than likely, his own inadequacy and his lack of understanding that had driven him to fear.

I am thinking like a man of flesh and bone, he told himself, *not like a disembodied brain. The flesh still clings to me; the bones will not dissolve.*

The scientist was still talking. *We must refrain especially,* he was saying, *from automatically thinking of the manifestation as something that had a mystical or a spiritual quality.*

It was just one of those simple things, said the grande dame, glad to get it settled.

We must keep firmly in our consciousness, said the scientist, *that there are no simple things in the universe. No happenings to be brushed casually to one side. There is a purpose in everything that happens. There always is a cause—you may be sure of that—and in time there will be effect as well.*

I wish, said the monk, *I could be as positive as you are.*

I wish, said the grande dame, *we hadn't landed on this planet. It is an ishy place.*

7

"YOU must restrain yourself," Nicodemus said. "Not too much. The vichyssoise, one small slice of roast, half of the potato. You must realize that your gut has been inactive for hundreds of years. Frozen, certainly, and subject to no deterioration, but, even so, it must be given an opportunity to get into tone again. In a few days you can resume normal eating habits."

Horton eyed the food. "Where did you get this fare?" he demanded. "Certainly it was not carried from Earth."

"I forget," said Nicodemus. "Of course you wouldn't know. We have on board the most efficient model of a matter converter that had been manufactured up to the time of our departure."

"You mean you just shovel in some sand?"

"Well, not exactly that. It isn't quite that simple. But you have the right idea."

"Now wait a minute," said Horton. "There is something very wrong. I don't remember any matter converters. They were talking about them, of course, and there seemed some hope that one could be put together, but to the best of my recollection . . ."

"There are certain things, sir," said Nicodemus, rather hurriedly, "with which you are not acquainted.

One of them is that once you went into cold-sleep, we did not leave immediately.''

"You mean there was some delay?''

"Well, yes. As a matter of fact, quite a bit of delay.''

"For Christ's sake, don't try to be mysterious about it. How long?''

"Well, fifty years or so.''

"Fifty years! Why fifty years? Why put us into cold-sleep and then wait fifty years?''

"There was no real urgency,'' said Nicodemus. "The time span of the project was estimated to run over so long a time, a couple of hundred years or perhaps slightly more before a ship returned with news of habitable planets, that a delay of fifty years did not seem excessive if in that length of time it was possible to develop certain systems that would give a better chance of success.''

"Like a matter converter, for example.''

"Yes, that was one of the things. Not absolutely necessary, of course, but convenient and adding a certain margin. There were, more importantly, certain ship engineering features which, if they could be worked out . . .''

"And they were worked out?''

"Most of them,'' said Nicodemus.

"They never told us there would be such delay,'' said Horton. "Neither us nor any of the other crews that were in training at the time. If any of the other crews had known, they'd gotten the word to us.''

"There was,'' said Nicodemus, "no need for you to know. There might have been some illogical objection on your part if you had been told. And it was important that the human crews be ready when the ships were set to go. You see, all of you were very special people.

Perhaps you remember with what great care you were chosen.''

"God, yes. We were run through computers for calculations of survival factors. Our psychological profiles were measured time and time again. They damn near wore us out with physical testing. And they implanted that telepathic dingus in our brains so we could talk with Ship, and that was the most bothersome of all. I seem to recall it took months to learn how to use it properly. But why do all this, then rush us to cold storage? We could simply have stood by.''

"That could have been one approach," said Nicodemus, "with you growing older by the year. Not exactly youth, but not too great an age, was one of the factors that went into the selection of the crews. There'd be little sense in sending oldsters out. Placed in cold-sleep, you did not age. Time was not a factor to you, for in cold-sleep time is not a factor. Doing it the way it was done, the crews were standing by, their facilities and abilities undimmed by the time it took to get other bugs ironed out. The ships could have gone when you were frozen, but by waiting fifty years, the ships' chances and your chances were considerably enhanced. The life-support systems for the brains were perfected to a point that would have been thought impossible fifty years before, the linkage between brains and ship were made more efficient and sensitive and almost foolproof. The cold-sleep systems were improved.''

"I have divided feelings about it," said Horton. "However, I guess it personally makes no difference to me. If you can't live out your life in your own time, I suppose it becomes immaterial when you do live it out. What I do regret is that I am left alone. Helen and I had something going for us, and I liked the other two. I

34

suppose, as well, there is some guilt because they died and I lived on. You say you saved my life because I was in cubicle number one. If I'd not been in it, one of the others would have lived and I would now be dead.''

"You must feel no guilt," Nicodemus told him. "If there is anyone who should feel the guilt, I am the one, but I feel no guilt, for reason tells me I was capable and performed to the limit of current technology. But you— you had no part in it. You did nothing; you shared in no decision.''

"Yes, I know. But, even so, I can't avoid thinking . . .''

"Eat your soup," said Nicodemus. "The roast is growing cold.''

Horton had a spoonful of the soup. "It is good," he said.

"Of course it is. I told you I can be an accomplished chef.''

"Can be," said Horton. "That's a strange way of putting it. You either *are* a chef, or you aren't. But you say you *can be* one. That was what you said about being an engineer. Not that you were one, but that you could be one. It seems to me, my friend, you can be too many things. A moment ago you implied that you were, as well, a good cold-sleep technician.''

"But the way I say it is precisely right," protested Nicodemus. "That is the way it is. I am a chef right now and can be an engineer or a mathematician or astronomer or geologist . . .''

"There's no need for you to be a geologist. I'm the geologist of this expedition. Helen was the biologist and chemist.''

"Some day," said Nicodemus, "there might be need of two geologists.''

"This is ridiculous," said Horton. "No man or no

35

robot could be as many things as you say you are or could be. It would take years of study, and in the process of learning each new specialty or discipline, you'd lose some of the previous training you had taken. Furthermore, you're simply a service robot, not specialized at all. Let's face it, your brain capacity is small, and your reaction system is comparatively insensitive. Ship said that you were chosen deliberately because of your simplicity—because there was very little that could go wrong with you."

"Which is all true enough," Nicodemus admitted. "I am what you say I am. A runner-of-errands and a fetcher-of-objects and good for little else. My brain capacity is small. But when you have two brains or three . . ."

Horton threw down his spoon on the table. "You are mad!" he said. "No one has two brains."

"I have," said Nicodemus calmly. "I have two brains right now—the old standard, stupid robot brain and a chef-brain and if I wanted, I could add another brain, although I do not know what kind of brain would supplement a chef-brain. A nutritionist-brain, perhaps, although the kit doesn't have that kind of brain."

With an effort, Horton controlled himself. "Now let's start over," he said. "Let's take it from the top and go slow and easy so that this stupid human brain of mine can follow what you're saying."

"It was those fifty years," said Nicodemus.

"What fifty years, goddammit?"

"Those fifty years they took after you were frozen. A lot of good research and development can be done in fifty years if a lot of humans put their minds to it. You trained, did you not, with a most accomplished robot— the finest piece of humanoid machinery that had ever been built."

36

"Yes, we did," said Horton. "I can remember him as if it were only yesterday . . ."

. "To you," said Nicodemus, "it would be only yesterday. The thousand years since then are as nothing to you."

"He was a little stinker," Horton said. "He was a martinet. He knew three times more than we did and was ten times as capable. He rubbed it into us in his suave, sleek, nasty way. So slick about it you could never peg him. All of us hated the little sonofabitch."

"There, you see," said Nicodemus triumphantly. "That could not continue. It was a situation that could not be tolerated. If he'd been sent with you, think of all the friction, the clash of personalities. That is why you have me. They couldn't use a thing like him. They had to use a simple, humble clod like me, the kind of robot you were accustomed to ordering around and who would not resent the ordering around. But a simple, humble clod like me would be incapable on his own to rise to the occasions that necessity sometimes might demand. So they hit upon the idea of auxiliary brains that could be plugged into place to supplement a cloddish brain like mine."

"You mean you have a box full of auxiliary brains that you just plug in!"

"Not really brains," said Nicodemus. "They are called transmogs, although I'm not sure why. Someone once told me the term was short for transmogrification. Is there such a word?"

"I don't know," said Horton.

"Well, anyhow," said Nicodemus, "I have a chef transmog and a physician transmog and a biochemist transmog—well, you get the idea. A full college course encoded in each of them. I counted them once, but now I have forgotten. A couple of dozen, I would guess."

"So you actually might be able to fix this tunnel of the Carnivore's."

"I wouldn't count on it," said Nicodemus. "I don't know what the engineer transmog contains. There are so many different kinds of engineering—chemical, mechanical, electrical."

"At least you'll have an engineering background."

"That's right. But the tunnel the Carnivore talked about probably wasn't built by humans. Humans wouldn't have had the time . . ."

"It could be human-built. They've had almost a thousand years to do a lot of things. Remember what the fifty years you've been talking about accomplished."

"Yeah, I know. You could be right. Relying on ships might not have been good enough. If the humans had relied on ships, they wouldn't have gotten out this far by now and . . ."

"They could have if they developed faster-than-light. Maybe once you develop that, there would be no natural limit. Once you break the light barrier, there might be no limit to how much faster than light you could go."

"Somehow I don't think they developed faster-than-light ships," said Nicodemus. "I listened to a lot of talk about it during that period after I was drafted into this project. No one seemed to have any real starting point, no real appreciation of what is involved. What more than likely happened is that humans landed on a planet not nearly as far out as we are now and found one of the tunnels and are now using the tunnels."

"But not only humans."

"No, that's quite apparent from Carnivore. How many other races may be using them we can have no

38

idea. What about Carnivore? If we don't get the tunnel operating, he'll want to ship with us."

"Over my dead body."

"You know, I feel pretty much the same. He's a rather uncouth personage and it might be quite a problem to put him into cold-sleep. Before we tried that, we'd have to know his body chemistry."

"Which reminds me that we're not going back to Earth. What is the scoop? Where does Ship intend to go?"

"I wouldn't know," said Nicodemus. "We talked off and on, of course. Ship, I am sure, tried to hold nothing back from me. I have the feeling Ship doesn't quite know itself what it intends to do. Just go, I suppose, and see what it can find. You realize, of course, that Ship, if it wishes to, can listen in on anything we say."

"That doesn't bother me," said Horton. "As it stands, we're all tied up in the same can of worms. You for much longer than will be the case with me. Whatever the situation, I suppose I'll have to stand upon it, for I have no other base. I'm close to a thousand years away from home, and a thousand years behind the Earth of this moment. Ship undoubtedly is right in saying that if I went back I would be a misfit. You can accept all of this intellectually, of course, but it gives you a strange feeling in the gizzard. If the other three were here, I imagine it would be different. I have the sense of being horribly alone."

"You aren't alone," said Nicodemus. "You have Ship and me."

"Yes, I suppose so. I seem to keep forgetting."

He pushed back from the table. "That was a fine dinner," he said. "I wish you could have eaten with me. Before I go off to bed, do you think it would disaccommodate my gut if I had a slice of that roast, cold?''

"For breakfast," said Nicodemus. "If you want a slice for breakfast."

"All right, then," said Horton. "There's still one thing that bothers me. With the setup that you have, you don't really need a human on this expedition. At the time I took the training, a human crew made sense. But not any longer. You and Ship could do the job alone. Given the situation as it is, why didn't they just junk us? Why did they bother putting us on board?''

"You seek to mortify yourself and the human race," said Nicodemus. "It is no more than shock reaction to what you have just learned. To start with, the idea was to put knowledge and technology on board, and the only way it could be put on board was in the persons of humans who had that knowledge and technology. By the time the ships took off, however, another means of supplying technology and knowledge had been found in the transmogs which could make even such simple robots as myself into multispecialists. But even so there would be, in us, still one factor lacking—that strange quality of humanness, the biological human condition which we still lack and which no roboticist has as yet been able to build into us. You spoke of your training robot and your hatred of him. This is what happens when you go beyond a certain point in robotic improvement. You gain good capability, but the humanity to balance the capability is lacking and the robot, instead of becoming more humanlike, becomes arrogant and insufferable. It may always be so. Humanity may be a factor that cannot be arrived at artificially. An expedition to the stars, I suppose, could function efficiently

40

with only robots and their transmog kits aboard, but it would not be a human expedition, and that is what this and the other expeditions were all about—to seek out planets where the people of Earth could live. Certainly the robots could make observations and reach decisions and nine times out of ten the observations would be accurate and the decisions quite correct, but in that tenth time, one or both could be wrong because the robots would be looking at the problem with robotic eyes and making the decisions with robotic brains that lacked that all important factor of the human quality.''

"Your words are comforting," said Horton. "I only hope you are right."

"Believe me, sir, I am."

Ship said, *Horton, you'd better get to bed now. The Carnivore will be coming to meet you in the morning, and you should get some sleep.*

8

BUT sleep came hard.

Lying on his back, staring up into the blackness, the strangeness and the loneliness came pouring in upon him, the strangeness and the loneliness that had been held off till now.

Only yesterday, Nicodemus had said to him. *It was only yesterday that you went into cold-sleep, because all the centuries that have come and gone since then mean less than nothing to you.*

It had been, he thought, with some surprise and bitterness, only yesterday. And now alone, to remember and to mourn. To mourn, here in the darkness of a planet far from Earth, arrived at, so far as he was concerned, in the twinkling of an eye, to find the home planet and the people of that yesterday sunk in the depths of time.

Helen dead, he thought. Dead and lying underneath the steely glitter of stranger stars on an unknown planet of an unrecorded sun, where the glaciers of frozen oxygen reared their bulk against the black of space and the primal rock lay uneroded through millennia piled upon millennia, a planet as unchanging as was death itself.

The three of them together—Helen, Mary, Tom. Only he was missing—missing because he had been in

42

cubicle number one, because a stupid, flat-footed, oaf-ish robot could think of no other system than doing a task by numbers.

Ship, he whispered in his mind.

Go to sleep, said Ship.

To hell with you, said Horton. *You can't baby me. You can't tell me what to do. Go to sleep, you say. Take a lead, you say. Forget it all, you say.*

We do not tell you to forget, said Ship. *The memory is a precious one, and while you must mourn, hold the memory fast. When you mourn, know that we mourn with you. For we remember Earth as well.*

But you won't go back to it. You plan to go on. After this planet, you plan to go on. What do you expect to find? What are you looking for?

There is no way of knowing. We have no expectations.

And I go with you?

Of course, said Ship. *We are a company, and you are part of it.*

The planet? We'll take time to look it over?

There is no hurry, said Ship. *We have all the time there is.*

What we felt this evening? That's a part of it? A part of this unknown that we're going to?

Good night, Carter Horton, said Ship. *We will talk again. Think of pleasant things and try to go to sleep.*

Pleasant things, he thought. Yes, there had been pleasantness back where the sky was blue, with white clouds floating in it, with a picture-ocean running its long fingers up and down a picture-beach, with Helen's body whiter than the sands they lay upon. There had been picnic fires with the night-wind moving through the half-seen trees. There had been candlelight upon a snow-white cloth, with gleaming china and sparkling glass set upon the table, with music in the background and contentment everywhere.

Somewhere in the outer darkness, Nicodemus moved clumsily about, trying to be quiet, and through the open port came a far-off strident fiddling of what he told himself were insects. If there were insects here, he thought.

He tried to think of the planet that lay beyond the port, but it seemed he could not think of it. It was too new and strange for him to think of it. But he found that he could conjure up the frightening concept of that vast, silent depth of space that lay between this place and Earth, and he saw in his mind's eye the tiny mote of Ship floating through that awesome immensity of nothingness. The nothingness translated into loneliness, and with a groan, he turned over and clutched the pillow tight about his head.

9

CARNIVORE showed up shortly after morning light.

"Good," he said. "You're ready. We travel in no hurry. Is not far to go. I checked the tunnel before I left. It had not fixed itself."

He led the way, up the sharp pitch of the hill, then down into a valley that lay so deep between the hills and was so engulfed in forest that the darkness of the night had not been dispelled entirely. The trees stood tall, with few branches for the first thirty feet or so, and Carter noted that while in general structure they were much like the trees of Earth, the bark tended to have a scaly appearance and the leaves mostly merged toward black and purple rather than to green. Underneath the trees, the forest floor was fairly open, with only an occasional scattering of spindly and fragile shrubs. At times, tiny skittering creatures scampered across the ground, which was littered with many fallen branches, but at no time did Carter manage to get a good look at them.

Here and there rock outcroppings thrust out of the hillside and when they descended another hill and crossed a small but brawling stream, low cliffs rose on the opposite bank. Carnivore led the way to where a path went up through a break in the wall of rock and they scrambled up the steep incline. Carter noted that the cliffs were pegmatite. There was no sign of sedimentary strata.

They scrambled up the cleft and emerged on a hill that rose to another ridge, higher than the other two they had crossed. At the top, a scatter of boulders and a low ledge of rock outcropping ran along the ridge. Carnivore sat down upon a slab of stone and patted a place beside him, inviting Horton to sit.

"Here we pause and catch the breath," he said. "The land is rugged hereabouts."

"How much farther?" Carter asked.

Carnivore waved a nest of tentacles that served him as a hand. "Two more hills," he said, "and we are almost there. Did you, by the way, catch god-hour last night?"

"God-hour?"

"Shakespeare called it that. Something reaching down and touching. Like someone being there."

"Yes," said Horton, "we caught it. Can you tell us what it is?"

"I do not know," said Carnivore, "and I do not like it. It look inside of you. It lay you open to the gut. That's why I left you so abruptly. It jitters me. It turns me into water. But I stayed too long. It caught me going home."

"You mean you knew that it was coming?"

"It comes every day. Or almost every day. There are times, not for very long, when it may not come at all. It moves across the day. It is coming now of evenings. It comes each time just a fraction later. It walks across the day and night. It keeps changing of its hour, but the change is very small."

"It's been coming all the time you've been here?"

"All the time," said Carnivore. "It does not leave one be."

"You have no idea what it is?"

"Shakespeare said it something out of space. He said it works like something far in space. It comes when this point of planet that we stand upon faces some point far in space."

Nicodemus had been prowling along the ledge of rock, stooping now and then to pick up a fallen chunk of stone. Now he came stalking toward them, holding out several small stones in his hand.

"Emeralds," he said. "Weathered out and lying on the ground. There are others in the matrix."

He handed them to Horton. Horton looked closely at them, holding them in the palm of his hand, probing at them with an index finger.

Leaning over, Carnivore had a look at them. "Pretty rocks," he said.

"Hell, no," said Horton. "More than pretty rocks. These are emeralds." He looked up at Nicodemus. "How did you know?" he asked.

"I am wearing my rockhound transmog," said the robot. "I put in my engineering transmog and there was room for one more, so I put in the rockhound . . ."

"Rockhound transmog! What the hell are you doing with a rockhound transmog?"

"Each of us," Nicodemus said sedately, "was allowed to include one hobby transmog. For our own personal gratification. There were stamp transmogs and chess transmogs and a lot of others, but I thought a rockhound transmog . . ."

Horton pushed about the emeralds. "You say there are others?"

"I would suggest," said Nicodemus, "that we have a fortune here. An emerald mine."

Carnivore rumbled, "What do you mean, a fortune?"

"He is right," said Horton. "This entire hill could be an emerald mine."

"There pretty rocks have value?"

"Among my people, a great deal of value."

"I never heard the like," said Carnivore. "Mad to me it sounds." He gestured with contempt at the emeralds. "Only pretty rocks, pleasing to the eye. But what to do with them?"

He rose slowly. "We go on," he said.

"All right, we'll go on," said Horton. He handed the emeralds to Nicodemus.

"But we should look around . . ."

"Later," Horton said. "They'll still be here."

"We'll need a survey, so that Earth . . ."

"Earth is no longer a consideration for any of us," said Horton. "You and Ship made that clear. No matter what happens, no matter what we find, Ship's not going back."

"You speak incomprehensible to me," said Carnivore.

"Forgive us," Horton told him. "It is a small private joke. Not worthy of explaining."

They went on down the hill and across another valley, then up another hill. This time there were no rest pauses. The sun rose higher and dispelled some of the forest gloom. The day grew warm.

Carnivore slouched along at a ground-gaining pace which seemed easy for him, with Horton puffing along behind him and Nicodemus bringing up the rear. Watching him, Horton tried to make up his mind what kind of creature Carnivore might be. He was a slob, of course—there was no doubt of that—but a vicious, killing slob that could be dangerous. He seemed friendly enough with his continual chatter about his old friend Shakespeare, but he would bear watching. So far he had given no indication of other than bluff good humor. There was no question that the affection he held for the human, Shakespeare, had been anything but geniune, although his talk of eating Shakespeare still rankled. His nonrecognition of the value of emeralds was a puzzling factor. It seemed impossible that any culture should fail to recognize the value of gemstones, unless it were a culture which had no concept of adornment.

From the last hill they had climbed, they went down, not into a valley, but into a cuplike depression rimmed by hills. Carnivore stopped so suddenly that Horton, walking behind him, bumped into him.

"There it be," said Carnivore, pointing. "You can see it from here. We almost are upon it."

Horton looked where he was pointing. He could see nothing but the forest.

"That white thing?" asked Nicodemus.

"That is it," said Carnivore, delighted. "That is it, the whiteness of it. I keep it clean and white, scrubbing off the tiny plants that essay to grow upon it, washing off the dust. Shakespeare called it Grecian. Can you tell me, sir or robot, what a Grecian is? I inquire of Shakespeare, but he only laugh and shake his head and say too long a story. I think at times he does not know himself. He only used a word he heard."

"Grecian comes from a human folk called Greeks," said Horton. "They achieved a greatness many centuries ago. A building built as they once built is called Grecian. It is a very general term. There are many factors to Grecian architecture."

"Simply built," said Carnivore. "Wall and roof and door. That is all it is. Good habitat to live in, though.

Tight to wind and rain. Do you not see it yet?''

Horton shook his head. "Soon you will," said Carnivore. "We be there very quickly."

They went on down the slope and at the bottom of it, Carnivore stopped again. He pointed to a path. "That way to home," he said. "That way, step or two, to spring. You want good drink of water?"

"I would," said Horton. "That was a strenuous hike. Not too far, but all up and down."

The spring gushed out of the hillside into a rock-rimmed pool, the water escaping from the pool to go trickling away in a tiny stream.

"You go ahead of me," said Carnivore. "You are guest of mine. Shakespeare said guests all go first. I was guest of Shakespeare. He was here ahead of me."

Horton knelt, and bracing his hands, lowered his head to drink. The water was so cold that it seemed to burn his throat. Sitting up, he squatted on his heels while Carnivore dropped to his four feet, lowered his head and drank—not really drinking, but lapping up the water as a cat would do.

For the first time, squatting there, Horton really saw and appreciated the somber beauty of the forest. The trees were thick and, even in the full sunlight, dark. While the trees were not conifers, the forest reminded him of the dark pine forests in the northlands of the Earth. Growing around the spring and extending up the slope down which they had come were clumps of shrubs, three feet or so in height, all blood-red in color. He could not recall that he had seen, anywhere, a single flower or blossom. He made a mental note to ask about that later.

Halfway up the path, Horton finally saw the building that Carnivore had attempted to point out to him. It stood upon a knoll in a small clearing. It did have a

Grecian look about it, although he had no background on Grecian or any other type of architecture. Small and constructed of white stone, its lines were severe and simple, but somehow it seemed to have a boxlike appearance. There was no portico, no fanciness at all—just four walls, an unadorned door, and a gable, not too high, with very little pitch.

"Shakespeare lived there when I come," said Carnivore. "I settled in with him. We spend happy time here. Planet is tail-end of nowhere, but happy comes inside you."

They crossed the clearing and came up to the building, walking three abreast. When they were a few feet from it, Horton glanced up and saw something he had missed before, the bleached whiteness of it lost in the whiteness of the stone. He stopped dead in horror. Affixed above the door was a human skull, grinning down at them.

Carnivore saw him staring at it. "Shakespeare bids us welcome," he said. "That is Shakespeare's skull."

Staring in fascination and horror, Horton saw that Shakespeare had two missing front teeth.

"Hard it was to fasten Shakespeare up there," Carnivore was saying. "Bad place to put him, for bone soon weather and be gone, but that was what he asked. Skull above the door, he told me, bones hung in sacks inside. I do it as he ask me, but it was sorrowful task. I do it with no liking, but a sense of duty and friendship."

"Shakespeare asked you to do this?"

"Yes, of course. You think I did it on my own?"

"I don't know what to think."

"Way of death," he said. "Eat him even as he dies. Priestly function, he explained. I do it as he say. I promise not to gag, and I do not gag. I harden me and

51

eat him, bad as he might taste, down to last scrap of gristle. I polish off his bones meticulously until none but bone remain. More than I want to eat. Belly full to bursting, but I keep on eating, never stopping until he all is gone. I do it right and proper. I do it with all holiness. I do not shame my friend. I was only friend he had.''

"It could be," said Nicodemus. "The human race can come up with some peculiar notions. One friend ingesting another friend as a gesture of respect. Among prehistoric people, there was ritual cannibalism—doing a true friend or a great man a special honor by the eating of him.''

"But what was prehistoric," Horton objected. "I never heard of a modern race . . ."

"A thousand years," said Nicodemus, "since we were upon the Earth. Plenty of time for the development of very strange beliefs. Maybe those prehistoric people knew something that we didn't. Maybe there was a logic to ritualistic cannibalism, and that logic was rediscovered in the last thousand years or so. Twisted logic, probably, but with appealing factors.''

"You say," Carnivore asked, "that your race do not do this? I do not understand.''

"A thousand years ago they didn't, but perhaps they do it now.''

"Thousand years ago?''

"We left Earth a thousand years ago. Perhaps a great deal more than a thousand years ago. We do not know the mathematics of time dilation. It could be a lot more than a thousand years.''

"But no human lives a thousand years.''

"True, but I was in cold-sleep. My body was frozen.''

"Frozen and you die.''

"Not the way we did it. Someday I'll explain."

"You think not ill of me for the eating of the Shakespeare?"

"No, of course we don't," said Nicodemus.

"That is well," said Carnivore, "for if you did you would not take me with you when you leave. Dearest wish I have is to get off this planet as soon as possible."

"We may be able to fix the tunnel," said Nicodemus. "If we are able to, you can leave by tunnel."

10

THE tunnel was a ten-foot square of mirrored blackness set into the face of a small dome of rock which thrust itself upward out of the underlying rock a short distance down the hill from the Grecian building. Between the building and the dome of rock ran a path worn down to rock and even, it seemed, worn into the very rock. There had been, at some time in the past, heavy traffic there.

Carnivore gestured at the mirrored blackness. "When it is working," he said, "it is not black, but shiny white. You walk into it, and on second step somewhere else you are. Now you walk into it and it shove you back. You cannot approach it. There is nothing there, but the nothing shove you back."

"But when it takes you somewhere," asked Horton, "when it's working, I mean, and will take you somewhere, how do you know where it is about to take you?"

"You don't," said Carnivore. "At one time, maybe, you say where you want to go, but not now. That machinery over there," he waved his arm, "that panel set beside the tunnel—it is possible, at one time, with it you could select your destination, but no one knows now how it operates. But it makes small difference, really. If you do not like the place you get to, you step back into it again and go otherwise. You always, after many times, perhaps, find some place that you like. For me, I'd be happy to go anywhere from here."

"That doesn't sound quite right," said Nicodemus.

"Of course it's not," said Horton. "The entire system must be out of kilter. No one in their right mind would build a nonselective transportation system. This way it could take you centuries to reach your destination—if you ever reached it."

"Very good," said Carnivore, placidly, "for being on the dodge. No one—not even self—knows where you will wind up. Maybe if pursuer sees you ducking into tunnel and ducks in after you, it may not take him to same place as you."

"You know this, or are you just guessing?"

"Guessing, I suppose. How is one to know?"

"The entire system's haywire," said Nicodemus, "if it works at random. You do not travel in it. You play a game with it, and the tunnel always wins."

"But this one takes you nowhere," wailed Carnivore. "I'm not picky where I go—anywhere but here. My fervent hope is that you can fix it so it takes me anywhere."

"I would suspect," said Horton, "that it was built millennia ago and has, for centuries, been abandoned by the ones who built it. Without proper maintenance, it has broken down."

"But that is not the point," protested Carnivore. "Point is, can you fix it?"

Nicodemus had moved over to the panel set into the rock beside the tunnel. "I don't know," he said. "I can't even read the instruments, if they are instruments. Some of them look like manipulative gadgets, but I can't be sure."

"It wouldn't harm to try and see what happens,"

Horton said. "You can't make the situation worse."

"But I can't," said Nicodemus. "I can't even reach them. There seems to be some sort of force field. Paper thin, perhaps, I can put my fingers on the instruments, or rather I think I have my fingers on them, but there's no contact. I don't really touch them. I can feel them underneath my fingers, but I'm not in actual contact with them. It is as if they were coated with a slippery grease."

He held up one hand and looked closely at it. "But there's not any grease," he said.

"The damn thing works one way," bawled Carnivore. "It should work two ways."

"Keep your shirt on," said Nicodemus shortly.

"You think you can do something with it?" asked Horton. "There's a force field there, you said. You could get yourself blown up. Do you know anything about force fields?"

"Not a thing," said Nicodemus cheerfully. "I didn't even know there could be such a thing. I just called it that. The term popped into my head. I don't know what it is."

He set down the toolbox he'd been carrying and knelt to open it. He began laying out tools on the rocky path:

"You got things to fix him with," crowed Carnivore. "Shakespeare had no tools. I have no goddamn tools, he'd say."

"A fat lot of good they'd done him even if he had them," said Nicodemus. "Even if you have them, you have to know how to use them."

"And you know how?" asked Horton.

"You're damn right I do," said Nicodemus. "I'm wearing this engineering transmog."

"Engineers don't use tools. It's mechanics who use tools."

"Don't bug me," said Nicodemus. "At the sight and feel of tools, it all falls into place."

"I can't bear to watch this," said Horton. "I think that I will leave. Carnivore, you spoke of a ruined city. Let's have a look at it."

Carnivore fidgeted. "But if he should need some help. Someone to hand him tools, perhaps. If he needs moral support . . ."

"I'll need more than moral support," said the robot. "I'll need great chunks of luck, and some divine intervention wouldn't hurt at all. Go and see your city."

11

By no stretch of the imagination was it a city. No more than a couple of dozen buildings, none of them large. They were oblong stone structures and had the look of barracks. The site lay half a mile or so from the building to which Shakespeare's skull was fastened, and stood on a slight rise of ground above a stagnant pond. Heavy brush and a scattering of trees had grown up between the buildings. In several instances, trees encroaching against the walls or corners of a building had dislodged or shifted some of the masonry. While most of the buildings were engulfed in the heavy growth, paths wandered here and there.

"Shakespeare chopped out the paths," said Carnivore. "He explored here and brought a few things home. Not much, only something now and then. Something that caught his fancy. He say we not disturb the dead."

"Dead?" asked Horton.

"Well, maybe too dramatic I make it sound. The gone, then, those who went away. Although that does not sound right either. How can one disturb those who have gone away?"

"The buildings all look alike," said Horton. "They look to me like barracks."

"Barracks is a word I do not have."

"A place to house a number of people."

"House? To live in?"

"That is right. At one time a number of people lived here. A trading post, perhaps. Barracks and warehouses."

"No one here to trade with."

"Well, okay, then—trappers, hunters, miners. There are the emeralds Nicodemus found. This place may be packed with gem-bearing formations or gravels. Or fur-bearing animals . . ."

"No fur-bearers," said Carnivore, positively. "Meat animals, that is all. Some low-grade predators. Nothing we must fear."

Despite the whiteness of the stone of which the buildings had been constructed, they gave the impression of dinginess, as if the buildings were no more than shacks. At the time they had been built, it was quite apparent that a clearing had been made, for despite the trees that had crept into the erstwhile clearing, the heavier forest still stood back. But, even with the sense of dinginess, there was a feel of solidity in the structures.

"They built to last," said Horton. "It was a permanent settlement of some sort, or intended to be permanent. It's strange that the building you and Shakespeare used was set apart from all the others. It could, I suppose, have been a guardhouse to keep an eye on the tunnel. Have you investigated these buildings?"

"Not me," said Carnivore. "They repel me. There is nastiness about them. Unsafeness. To enter one of them is like entering a trap. Close up on me, I would expect it, so I could not get out. Shakespeare poked around in them, to my nervousness. He bring a few small objects out of which he was fascinated. Although, as I tell you, he disturb but little. He said it should be left for others of his kind who knew of such things.''

''Archaeologists.''

''That's the word I search for. It escape my tongue. Shakespeare said shameful thing to mess up for archaeologists. They learn much from it where he learn nothing.''

''But you said . . .''

''A few small objects only. Easy to the hand. Small, he said, to carry and perhaps of value. He say you must not spit in the eye of fortune.''

''What did Shakespeare think this place might be?''

''He had many thoughts about it. Mostly, he wonders after heavy thought, if it not be place for malefactors.''

''You mean a penal colony.''

''He did not, to my remembrance, use the word you say. But he speculate a place to keep those not wanted otherwhere. He figure maybe tunnel never meant to operate but one way. Never two-way, always one-way tunnel. So those sent here never could go back.''

''It makes sense,'' said Horton. ''Although it wouldn't have to be. If the tunnel were abandoned in the ancient past, it would have been a long time without maintenance and would progressively have broken down. What you say about not knowing where you're going when you enter a tunnel and two people entering it and winding up at different destinations sounds wrong, too. A haphazard transportation system is impractical. Under a condition such as that, it seems unlikely the tunnel would have been widely used. What I can't understand is why people such as you and

Shakespeare should have used the tunnels."

"Tunnels only used," Carnivore said blithely, "by those who do not give a damn. Only by those who have no really choice. Go to places that make no sense to go to. All planet tunnels lead to are planets you can live on. Air to breathe. Not too hot, too cold. Not kind of places that kill you dead. But many worthless places. Many places where there is no one, maybe never been anyone."

"The people who built the tunnels must have had a reason to go to so many planets, even to those planets you call worthless. It would be interesting to find out their reasons."

"Only ones can tell you," said Carnivore, "are the ones who fabricate the tunnels. They gone. They somewhere else or nowhere at all. No one knows who they were or where to look for them."

"But some of the tunnel worlds are inhabited. Inhabited by people, I mean."

"Is so if definition of people is a very broad one and not too fussy. On many tunnel planets, trouble can come fast. Last one I was on, next to this, trouble comes not only fast, but big."

They had been walking slowly down the paths that wound among the buildings. Ahead of them the heavy underbrush closed in to obliterate the path. The path ended just beyond a door that opened into one of the structures.

"I'm going in," said Horton. "If you don't want to, wait outside for me."

"I'll wait," said Carnivore. "Inside of them makes a crawling on my spine, a jumping in my belly."

The inside of the place was dark. There was a dampness and a mustiness in the air and a chill that struck to the bone. Tensed, Horton felt the urge to leave, to duck back into sunlight once again. There was an alienness here that could be felt, but not defined—the feeling of being in a place where he had no right to be, a sense of intruding on something that should be kept darkly hidden.

Consciously planting his feet firmly, he stayed, although he felt the beginning of shivers up and down his back. Gradually his eyes grew accustomed to the gloom and he could make out shapes. Against the wall to his right stood what could be nothing else but a wooden cupboard. It was rickety with age. Horton had the feeling that if it were bumped, it would come tumbling down. The doors were held closed by wooden buttons. Beside the cupboard stood a wooden four-legged bench with great cracks running across its top. On the bench stood a piece of pottery—a water jug, perhaps, with a triangular piece broken from the rim. On the opposite end stood what looked like a vase. It certainly wasn't pottery. It looked like glass, but the layer of fine dust that covered everything made it impossible to tell with any surety. And beside the bench stood what had to be a chair. There were four legs, a seat, a slanted back. Hanging on one of the uprights of the back was a piece of fabric that could have been a hat. On the floor in front of the chair lay what seemed to be a plate—an oval of ceramic whiteness, and upon the plate, a bone.

Something, Horton told himself, had sat in the chair—how many years ago?—with a plate upon its lap, eating a joint of meat, perhaps holding the joint in its hands, or whatever served it for hands, chewing off the bone, with the water jug close at hand, although perhaps not water, but a jug of wine. And having finished with the joint, or eaten all it wanted of it, had placed the plate upon the floor, perhaps, as it did so, settling back and patting the fullness of its belly with some satisfaction. Putting the plate with the joint upon it down upon the floor, but then never coming back to pick up the plate. With no one ever coming back to pick up the plate.

He stood in fascination, staring at the bench, the chair, the plate. Some of the alienness seemed to have gone away, for here was a set piece snatched out of the past of a people who, whatever may have been their shape, held some of the elements of a common humanity that might extend throughout the universe. A midnight snack, perhaps—and what had happened once the midnight snack were eaten?

The chair to sit in, the bench to hold the jug, the plate to hold the joint—and the vase, what about the vase? It consisted of a globular body, a long neck, and a broad base for sitting. More like a bottle than a vase, he thought.

He stepped forward and reached out for it and as he reached brushed against the hat, if it were a hat, that hung upon the chair. At his touch, the hat disintegrated. It disappeared in a small puff of dust that floated in the air.

His hand grasped the vase or bottle and he lifted it and saw that the globular body of it was incised with pictures and symbols. Holding it by the neck, he brought it close up to his face so that he could see the decorations.

A strange creature stood within an enclosure that had a peaked roof with a little ball on top the roof. It looked for all the world, he thought, as if the creature stood inside a kitchen canister that might be used for storing tea. And the creature—was it humanoid or simply an animal standing on two sticklike hind legs? It had only one arm and it bore a heavy tail which extended at an upward angle to its upright body. The head was a blob, but extending upward and outward from it were six straight lines; three to the left, two to the right and one extending straight upward.

Twirling the bottle (or the vase?), other etchings came into view—horizontal lines formed within two lines, one above the other and seemingly attached to one another by vertical lines. Buildings, he wondered, with the vertical lines representing pillars supporting the roof? There were many squiggles and lopsided ovals and some irregular markings in short rows that could have been words in an unknown language. And what could have been a tower, from the top of which emerged three figures that had the look of foxes snatched from some old legend out of Earth.

From the path outside, Carnivore was calling to him, "Horton, all goes well with you?"

"Very well," said Horton.

"I apprehensive for you," said Carnivore. "Please, will you not come out? You make me nervous, staying."

"All right," said Horton, "since it makes you nervous."

He turned about and went out the door, still carrying the bottle.

"You find a receptacle of interest," said Carnivore, eyeing it with some misgiving.

"Yes, look here." Horton lifted the bottle, turning it slowly. "Representations of some sort of life, although I'm hard put to tell exactly what they were."

"Shakespeare found a couple similar. With markings on them also, but not exact as yours. He also puzzled hard over what they were."

"They could be representations of the people who lived here."

"Shakespeare said the same, but qualified his saying to their being only myths of people who were here. He explain that myths are racial rememberings, things that memory, often faulty, says happened in the past." He fidgeted nervously. "Leave us return," he said. "My belly growls for nourishment."

"And so does mine," said Horton.

"I have meat. Killed only yesterday. You will join me at my meat?"

"Most gladly," Horton said. "I have rations, but not as good as meat."

"Meat is not as yet too high," said Carnivore. "But I kill again tomorrow. Like meat on the fresh side. Eat it high only in emergency. I suppose you subject your meat to fire, same as Shakespeare did."

"Yes, I like it cooked."

"Dry wood there is in plenty for the fire. Stacked outside the house and waiting for the blaze. Have a hearth for fire out front. I suppose you saw it."

"Yes, I saw the hearth."

"The other. Does he eat meat as well?"

"He does not eat at all."

"Unbelievable," said Carnivore. "How does he keep his strength?"

"He has what you call a battery. It supplies him food of a different sort."

"You think this Nicodemus not fix tunnel right away? Back there, you seem to be saying that."

"I think it might take a while," said Horton. "He

has no idea what it is about and neither of us can help him.''

They went back along the winding path they'd followed.

''What is that smell?'' asked Horton. ''Like something dead, or worse.''

''It is the pond,'' said Carnivore. ''The pond you must have noticed.''

''I saw it coming in.''

''It smell most obnoxiously,'' said Carnivore. ''Shakespeare call it Stinking Pond.''

12

HORTON squatted before the fire, superintending the cut of meat roasting over the coals. Carnivore sat across the fire from him, tearing with his teeth at the slab of raw meat he held. Blood smeared his muzzle and ran down his face.

"You do not mind?" he asked. "My stomach aches exceedingly for filling."

"Not at all," said Horton. "Mine will be just a minute more."

The sun of late afternoon was warm against his back. The heat of the fire beat against his face and he found himself exulting in the comfort of the camp. The fire was placed directly in front of the snow-white building, with Shakespeare's skull grinning down upon them. Heard in the silence was the gurgle of the stream that ran below the spring.

"Once we are done," said Carnivore, "I show to you the possessions of the Shakespeare. I have them all neatly bagged. You have interest in them?"

"Yes, of course," said Horton.

"In many ways," said Carnivore, "the Shakespeare was an aggravating human, although I like him dearly. I never really knew if he liked me or not, although I think he did. We got along together. We work very well together. We talk a lot together. We tell each other many things. But I never can erase the feeling he was laughing at me, although why he should I do not understand. Do you find me funny, Horton?''

"Not in the least," said Horton. "You must have imagined it."

"Can you tell me what *goddamn* means? The Shakespeare always using it and I fall into habit with him. But I never knew what it means. I ask him what is it and he would not tell. He only laugh at me, deep inside himself."

"It has no real meaning. Ordinarily, I mean. It is used for emphasis, with no real import of meaning. It is a saying only. Most people do not use it habitually. Only some of them. Others use it sparingly and only under emotional provocation."

"It means nothing then. Only a way of speaking."

"That is right," said Horton.

"When I talk of magic, he call it goddamn foolishness. It does not mean, then, any special kind of foolishness."

"No, he just meant foolishness."

"You think magic foolishness?"

"I am not prepared to say. I guess I've never thought too much about it. I would suggest that magic lightly used might be foolishness. Perhaps magic is something no one understands. Do you have faith in magic? Do you practice magic?"

"My people have great magic through the years. Sometimes it works, sometimes not. I say to the Shakespeare let us put our magic together, maybe it will work to open up the tunnel. Shakespeare then say magic goddamn foolishness. He said that he had none. He said no such thing as magic."

"I suspect," said Horton, "that he spoke from

prejudice. You can't condemn something you know nothing of."

"Yes," said Carnivore, "the Shakespeare would do a thing like that. Although I think he lied to me. I think he used his magic. He had a thing that he called *book*, he said it Shakespeare book. It could talk to him. What is that but magic?"

"We call it *reading*," Horton said.

"He held the book and it talked to him. Then he talked to it. He makes little marks upon it with a special stick he have. I ask him what he do and he grunt at me. He was always grunting at me. Grunt meant leave him be, do not pester him."

"You have this book of his?"

"I'll show it to you later."

The steak was done, and Horton fell to eating.

"This is good," he said. "What kind of animal?"

"Not too big," siad Carnivore. "Not hard to kill. Does not try to fight. Get away is all. But toothsome. Many animals for meat, but this one most tasty of them all."

Nicodemus came stumping up the path, toolbox clutched in hand. He sat down beside Horton.

"Before you ask," he said, "I haven't got it fixed."

"But progress made?" asked Carnivore.

"I don't know," said Nicodemus. "I think I know how I may be able to get the force field disconnected, although I can't be sure. It is worth at least a try. Mostly I've been trying to figure out what's behind that force field. I drew all sorts of sketches and I tried some diagramming to gain an understanding of what it's all about. I have some ideas there, as well, but it all goes for nothing if I can't get the force shield off. And I may be wrong, of course, about everything."

"Not discouraged though?"

"No, I'll keep on trying."

"That is good," said Carnivore.

He swallowed the last hunk of his dripping gob of meat.

"I go down to spring," he said, "and wash my face. I am sloppy eater. You wish I wait for you?"

"No," said Horton. "I'll go down a little later. I still have eaten only half the steak."

"You excuse me, please," said Carnivore, getting to his feet. The other two sat watching him as he went loping down the trail.

"How did it go?" asked Nicodemus.

Horton shrugged. "There's a deserted village of sorts just east of here. Stone buildings overgrown with brush. No one's been there for centuries, from the looks of it. Nothing to show why they might have been here, or why they might have left. Carnivore says Shakespeare thinks it may have been a penal colony. If so, a neat way of doing it. With the tunnel inoperative, there'd be no need to fret about escapes."

"Does Carnivore know what kind of people?"

"He doesn't know. I don't think he cares. He has no real curiosity. The here and now is all that interests him. Besides, he's afraid of it. The past seems to terrify him. My guess is they were humanoids—not necessarily people as we think of them. I went into one of the buildings and found some kind of bottle. Thought it was a vase at first, but I guess it is a bottle."

He reached down beside him and handed the bottle to Nicodemus. The robot turned it over and over in his hands.

"Crude," he said. "The pictures may be only

approximately representational. Hard to tell what they represent. Some of this stuff looks like writing.''

Horton nodded. ''All true, but it means they had some idea of art. That could argue a culture on the move.''

''Not good enough,'' said Nicodemus, ''to account for the sophisticated technology of the tunnels.''

''I didn't mean to imply these were the people who built the tunnels.''

''Has Carnivore said anything further about joining us when we leave?''

''No. Apparently he is confident you can fix the tunnel.''

''Perhaps it's best not to tell him, but I'm not. I never saw such a mess as that control panel.''

Carnivore came waddling up the path.

''All clean now,'' he said. ''I see you're finished. How did you like the meat?''

''It was excellent,'' said Horton.

''Tomorrow we'll have fresh meat.''

''We'll bury the meat left over while you are on the hunt,'' said Horton.

''No need to bury it. Dump it in the pond. Holding nose most securely in process of doing it.''

''That's what you've been doing with it?''

''Sure,'' said Carnivore. ''Easy way to do it. Something in the pond that eats it up. Probably glad I throw it meat.''

''You ever see this thing that eats the meat?''

''No, but meat is gone. Meat floats in water. Meat thrown in pond never floats. Must be eaten.''

''Maybe your meat is what makes the pond stink.''

''Not so,'' said Carnivore. ''Always stink like that. Even before the throwing of the meat. The Shakespeare

71

here before me and he was throwing of no meat. Yet he said it stinks from the time he come."

"Stagnant water can smell pretty bad," said Horton, "but I never smelled it this bad."

"It may not be really water," said Carnivore. "It is thicker than water. Runs like water, looks like water, but not as thin as water. Shakespeare called it soup."

Long shadows, extending from the stand of trees to the west, had crept across the camp. Carnivore cocked his head, squinting at the sun.

"The god-hour is almost here," he said. "Leave us go inside. Beneath a stout stone it is not too bad. Not like in the open. Still feel it, but stone filters out the worst."

The interior of the Shakespeare house was simple. The floor was paved with slabs of stone. There was no ceiling; the single room was open to the roof. In the center of the room stood a large stone table and around the room ran a chair-high ledge of stone.

Carnivore gestured at it. "For sitting and for sleeping. Also place to put things."

The ledge in the rear of the room was crowded with jars and vases, weird pieces of what seemed to be small statuary, and other pieces for which, at first glance, there seemed to be no name.

"From the city," said Carnivore. "Objects that Shakespeare brought back from the city. Curious, perhaps, but of value slight."

A misshapen candle stood on one end of the table, stuck to the stone by its own drippings. "It gives the light," said Carnivore. "Shakespeare fashioned it of fat of the meat I killed so he could use it to pore over book—sometimes it talking to him, sometimes, with his magic stick, he talking back to it."

"This was the book," asked Horton, "that you told me I could see."

"Most certainly," said Carnivore. "You may, perhaps, explain it to me. Tell me what it is. I ask the Shakespeare many times but the explanation that he gave me was no really explanation. I sit and eat my heart out to know and he would never tell. But tell me one thing, please. Why did ne need a light to talk with book?"

"It's called *reading*," Horton said. "The book talks by the marks upon it. You must have light to see the marks. For it to talk, the marks must be plainly seen."

Carnivore shook his head. "Strange goings-on," he said. "You humans are strange business. The Shakespeare strange. He always laughing at me. Not outside laughter, inside laughter. I like him, but he laugh. He makes laughter so he be better than I am. He laugh most secretly, but he lets me know he laughs."

He strode to a corner and picked up a bag fashioned out of an animal skin. He hoisted it in one fist and shook it and a dry rustling and scraping came out of it.

"His bones!" he shouted. "He laughs now only with his bones. Even the bones still laugh. Listen and you hear them."

He shook the bag viciously. "Do you not hear the laughter?"

The god-hour struck.

It still was a monstrous thing. Despite the thick stone walls and the ceiling, its force was not greatly diminished. Once again, Horton found himself seized and laid bare and open, to be explored and this time, it seemed, more than explored, but absorbed as well, so that it seemed, even as he struggled to remain himself, he became one with whatever it was that had seized

73

upon him. He felt the fusing with it, the becoming part of it and when he knew there was no way to fight against the fusing, tried despite his humiliation at being made a part of something else to do some probing of his own and thus find out what it was he was being made a part of. For an instant he thought he knew; for a single, fleeting instant, the thing that he had been absorbed by, the thing that he had become, seemed to reach out to take in the universe, everything that ever had been, or was, or would be, showing it to him, showing him the logic, or the nonlogic, the purpose, the reason and the goal. But in that instant of knowing, his human mind rebelled against the implication of the knowing, aghast and outraged that there could be such a thing as this, that the showing of the universe and the understanding of it might be possible. His mind and body wilted, preferring not to know.

How long it lasted he had no way of gauging. He hung limply in the grasp of it and it seemed to absorb not only him but his sense of time as well—as if it could manipulate time in its own fashion and for its own purposes, and he had a fleeting thought that if it could do this, there might be nothing that could stand against it, since time was the most elusive factor in the universe.

Finally it was over, and Horton was surprised to find himself crouched upon the floor, his arms up to cover his head. He felt Nicodemus lifting him, putting him on his feet and holding him erect. In anger at his helplessness, he struck the robot's hands away and staggered to the great stone table, clutching at it desperately.

"It was bad again," said Nicodemus.

Horton shook his head, trying to clear his brain. "Bad," he said. "As bad as it was before. And you?"

"The same as before," said Nicodemus. "A glancing mental blow was all. It works its will more harshly upon a biologic brain."

Through the fog, Horton heard Carnivore declaiming. "Something up there," he was saying, "seems interested in us."

13

HORTON opened the book to the title page. Beside his elbow the homemade candle guttered smokily, throwing a flickering and uncertain light. He bent close to read. The typeface was unfamiliar, and the words seemed wrong.

"What is it?" Nicodemus asked.

"I think it's Shakespeare," Horton told him. "What else could it be? But the spelling is all different. Strange abbreviations. And some of the letters wrong. Yes, look here—that would be it. *The Complete Works of William Shakespeare*. That's how I make it out. Do you agree with me?"

"But there's no publication date," said Nicodemus, leaning over Horton's shoulder.

"After our time, I would imagine," Horton said. "Language and spelling change as time goes on. No date, but published at—can you make out the word?"

Nicodemus bent his head closer. "London. No, not London. Someplace else. No place I ever heard of. Maybe not on Earth."

"Well, we know it's Shakespeare, anyhow," said Horton. "That's how come his name. He meant it as a joke."

Carnivore grumbled at them from across the table. "The Shakespeare full of jokes."

Horton turned the page, to a blank page filled with crabbed pencil script. He bent above the page, puzzling it out. It was composed, he saw, of the same odd spelling and word arrangement that he'd found on the title page. Tortuously, he made out the first few lines, translating them almost as he would have a foreign language:

If you are reading this, there is a probability you may have fallen in with that great monster, Carnivore. If such should be the case, don't, for an instant, trust the miserable sonofabitch. I know he intends to kill me, but I shall have the last laugh on him. The last laugh is an easy thing for one who knows that, in any case, he is about to die. The inhibitor I carried with me is all but gone by now, and once I have no more of it, the malignancy will continue to eat into my brain. And I am convinced, before the final killing pain sets in, it would be an easier death for this slobbering monster to kill me than it would be to die in pain . . .

"What does it say?" asked Nicodemus.

"I'm not sure," said Horton. "I have difficulty with it."

He pushed the book aside.

"He talked to book," said Carnivore, "with his magic stick. He never tell me what he said. You cannot tell me either?"

Horton shook his head.

"Able you should be," insisted Carnivore. "You human just like he. What one says with stick-marks the other one should know."

"It's the time factor," said Horton. "We've been upon our way at least a thousand years to reach here.

Perhaps a great deal more than a thousand years. In a thousand years or less there would be many changes in the symbols that the marking stick would make. Also, his inscription of the symbols are not of the best. He writes in a shaky hand.''

"You will try again? Great curiosity to know what the Shakespeare say, especially what he say of me.''

"I will keep on trying,'' Horton said.

He pulled the book back in front of him.

. . . die in pain. He pretends great friendship for me, and he carries his role so well that it requires considerable analytical effort to discern his actual attitude. To arrive at an understanding of him, one must first learn what kind of thing he is and gain an acquaintance of his background and his motivation. It was only slowly that I came to a realization that he is, in truth, what he seems to be and what he boasts he is—not only a confirmed carnivore, but a predator as well. Killing is not only a way of life for him; it is a passion and religion. Not he alone, but his very culture, is based upon the art of killing. Bit by bit I have been able, through a deep insight gained from living with him, to piece together the story of his life and background. If you should ask him, I should imagine that he would tell you, proudly, he is of a warrior race. But that does not tell the entire story. He is, among his race, a very special creature, by his own light perhaps a legendary hero—or at least about to become a legendary hero. His life profession, as I understand it (and I am sure my understanding is correct), is to travel world to world and on each world challenge and kill the most deadly species that has evolved upon it. In the manner of the legendary North American Indians of Old Earth, he counts symbolic coup for each adversary that he kills and, as I understand it, he now is runner-up in the entire history of his race and yearns most worthily to become the all-time champion, the greatest killer of them all. What this will gain him I'm not certain, but can only speculate—perhaps the immortality of racial memory, being enshrined forever in his tribal pantheon . . .

"Well?" asked Carnivore.

"Yes?"

"The book now talks to you. You move the finger, line by line."

"Nothing," said Horton. "Really nothing. Mostly prayers and incantations."

"I knew it," rasped Carnivore. "I knew it. He say my magic goddamn foolishness, and yet he practice of his own. He does not mention me? You sure he does not mention me?"

"Not yet. Perhaps a little farther on."

But in this abomination of a planet he is trapped with me. He is barred, as I am, from those other worlds wherein he could seek out and battle and destroy, to the eternal glory of his race, the most puissant life-forms he can ferret out. In consequence, I am sure I can detect in the great warrior mentality of him a quietly growing desperation, and I feel certain that the time will come when all hope is gone of other worlds, that he will make me the last name on his victory roll, although, God knows, the killing of me will be small credit to him, for I would be hopelessly outmatched. By indirection, I have done my best to impress upon him, in many subtle ways, what a frail and feeble opponent I would be. In my weakness, I had thought, lay my only hope. But now I know I am wrong. I can see the madness and the desperation grow upon him. If it goes on, I know one day he will kill me. At that time when his madness serves to magnify me into a foeman worthy of him, he'll have at me. Just what this will profit him, I do not know. It would seem there would be little point in killing when others of his race will not, cannot, know of it. But I somehow gain the impression, from what I do not know, that even in his present situation of being lost among the stars, the killing would be known and celebrated by others of his race. This is far beyond my understanding, and I have given up trying for an understanding of it.

He sits across the table from me as I write and I can see him measuring me, knowing full well, of course, that I am no worthy subject of his ritualistic killing pattern, but still trying to psych himself into believing that I am. Someday he will do it, and that will be the day. But I have him beat hands down. I have an ace tucked up my sleeve. He does not know that within me lies a death that has only a short time now to run. I shall be ripe to die before he is ready for the killing. And since he is a sentimental slob—all killers are sentimental slobs—I shall talk him into killing me as a priestly office, for the performance of which I turn to him in my greatest need as the only one who can perform this deed of ultimate compassion. So I shall do two things: I shall use him to cut short the final agony which I know must come, and I shall rob him of his final killing since killing done in mercy will not count for him. He shall not count coup upon me. Rather, I'll count coup on him. And as he kills me, mercifully, I shall laugh full in his face. For laughter is the final victory. Killing for him, laughter for me. This is the measurement between us.

Horton lifted his head and sat in stunned silence. The man was mad, he told himself. Mad, with a cold, icy, congealed madness that was far worse than raving madness. Not mere madness of the mind, but madness of the soul.

"So," said Carnivore, "he finally mentioned me."

"Yes. He said you are a sentimental slob."

"That do not sound so good."

"It is," said Horton, "a term of great affection."

"You are sure of that?" asked Carnivore.

"Very sure," said Horton.

"Then the Shakespeare really loved me."

"I am certain that he did," said Horton.

He went back to the book, rifling through the pages. *Richard III. The Comedy of Errors. The Taming of the Shrew. King John. Twelfth Night. Othello. King Lear. Hamlet.* They all were there. And scribbled on the margins, inscribed on the partially blank pages where plays came to an end, was the crabbed writing.

"He talked to it a lot," said Carnivore. "Almost every night. Sometimes on rainy days when we stayed inside."

All's Well That Ends Well, page 1038, scribbled on the left-hand margin:

The pond stinks the worst today I've ever smelled it. It is an evil smell. Not just a bad smell, but an evil smell. As if it were alive, exuding evil. As if it hid in its depth some obscenity . . .

King Lear, page 1143, the right-hand margin this time:

I found emeralds, weathered out of a ledge a mile or so below the spring. Just lying there, waiting to be picked up. I filled my pockets with them. I don't know why I bothered. Here I am, a rich man, and it doesn't mean a thing . . .

Macbeth, page 1207, bottom margin:

There is something in the houses. Something to be found. A riddle to be answered. I don't know what it is, but I feel it there . . .

Pericles, page 1381, on the lower half of the page left blank as the text came to an end:

We all are lost in the immensity of the universe. Having lost our home, we have no place to go or, what is worse, too many places to go. We are lost not only in the depths of our universe, but in the depths of our minds as well. When men stayed on one planet, they knew where they were. They had yardsticks for measurement and thumbs to test the weather. But now, even when we think we know where we are, we still are lost; for there is either no path to lead us home, or, in many cases, we have no home to which it is worth our while returning.

No matter where home may be, men today, at least intellectually, are footloose wanderers. Even though we may call a planet 'home,' even the few who still remain who can call the Earth their home, there is now no such thing as home. The human race now is fragmented to the stars, still scattering to the stars. We, as a race, are impatient with the past, and many of us with the present and we have only one direction, futureward, which takes us ever farther from the concept of home. As a race, we are incurable wanderers and we want nothing that will tie us down and nothing to hang onto—until that day which must come at some time to each of us, when we realize we're not as free as we think we are, but, rather, lost. It is only when we try to recall, with our racial memory, where we've been and why we've been there, that we realize the full measure of our lostness.

On one planet, or even in a single solar system, we could orient ourselves at the psychological center of the universe. For we had values then, values that we now see were limited, but at least values that provided a human framework within which we moved and lived. But that framework now is shattered, and our values have been splintered so many times by the different worlds we have trod upon (for each new world would give us either new values or negate some of the old ones to which we'd clung) that we have no basis upon which to form and exercise our judgments. We now have no scale upon which we can agree to delineate our losses or our aspirations. Even infinity and eternity have become concepts that differ in certain important ways. Once we used our science to structure the place in which we lived, to give it shape and reason; now we are confused because we have learned so much (although only a little of what there is to learn) that we cannot bring human scientific viewpoints to bear upon the universe as we see it now. We have more questions now then we ever had before, and less chance of finding answers. Provincial we may have been; there is no one who will deny that. But it must occur to many of us that in provincialism we found a comfort and a certain sense of safety. All life is set within an environment that is far greater than life itself, but given a few million years any kind of life can gain from its environment enough familiarity that it can live with its surroundings. But we, in leaving Earth, in spurning the planet of our birth for brighter, farther stars, have enlarged our environment enormously, and we do not have those few million years; in our haste we have no time at all.

The writing came to an end. Horton closed the book and shoved it to one side.

"Well?" asked Carnivore.

"Nothing," Horton said. "Just endless incantations. I do not understand them."

14

HORTON lay beside the fire, wrapped in his sleeping bag. Nicodemus moved about, putting more wood on the fire, his dark metal hide shot with glints of red and blue from the flicker of the flames. Above, the unfamiliar stars gleamed brightly, and down by the spring, something was complaining bitterly.

Horton settled himself more comfortably, feeling sleep stealing in upon him. He closed his eyes, not too tightly, and settled down to wait.

Carter Horton, said Ship, speaking in his mind.

Yes, said Horton.

I sense an intelligence, said Ship.

Carnivore? asked Nicodemus, crouched beside the fire.

No, not Carnivore. We would know Carnivore, having encountered him before. His intelligence pattern is not exceptional, is not greatly different from ours. This one is. Stronger and more keen, sharper, and somehow very different, but fuzzed and indistinct. As if it is an intelligence that is trying to stay hidden and escape attention.

Nearby? asked Horton.

Nearby. Close to where you are.

There is nothing here, said Horton. *The settlement is deserted. We've seen nothing all day long.*

If it were in hiding, you would not see it. You must remain alert.

The pond, perhaps, said Horton. *There may be something living in the pond. Carnivore seems to think there is. He thinks it eats the meat he throws in the pond.*

Perhaps, said Ship. *We seem to remember Carnivore saying the pond was not really water, more like soup. You've not been near it?*

It stinks, said Horton. *One does not go near it.*

We cannot pinpoint the intelligence, said Ship, *except that we know it's in your general area. Not too far away. Perhaps hidden. Take no chances. You wear your sidearms?*

Yes, of course we do, said Nicodemus.

That is good, said Ship. *Stay watchful.*

All right, said Horton. *Good night, Ship.*

Not yet, said Ship. *There is one thing. When you read the book, we tried to follow you, but could not make out all of what you read. This Shakespeare—Carnivore's friend, not the ancient playwright—what about him?*

A human, said Horton. *There can't be any doubt of that. His skull, at least, is human and his writing seems to be authentic human writing. But there was a madness in him. Perhaps engendered by malignancy, a brain tumor, more than likely. He wrote of an inhibitor, a cancer inhibitor, I suppose, but said he was running out of it and knew that once he did, he would die in terrible pain. That's why he tricked Carnivore into killing him, laughing all the while.*

Laughing?

He laughed all the time at Carnivore. Letting Carnivore know he was laughing at him. Carnivore speaks of it often. He was deeply hurt by it and it weighs upon his mind. I thought at first that this Shakespeare was a smart-ass—you know, someone with an inferiority complex which demanded that somehow, at no danger to himself, he must continually feed his ego. One way to do that is to engage in secret laughter at others, bearing out the fiction of a self-conceived and illusory superiority. I thought that at first, I say. Now I think the man was mad. He was suspicious of Carnivore. He thought Carnivore was about to kill him. Convinced that Carnivore would finally do him in.

And Carnivore? What do you think?

He's all right, said Horton. *There's no great harm in him.*

Nicodemus, what do you think?

I agree with Carter. He's no threat to us. I been meaning to tell you—we found an emerald mine.

We know, said Ship. *Note has been made of it. Although we suspect there'll be nothing come of it. We are not now concerned with emerald mines. Although, once this is done, it might do no harm to bring back a bucketful of them. No one knows. They might, somewhere, sometime come in handy.*

We'll do that, Nicodemus said.

And now, said Ship, *good night, Carter Horton. Nicodemus, you keep good watch while he sleeps.*

I intend to, said Nicodemus.

Good night, Ship, said Horton.

15

NICODEMUS shook Horton awake. "We have a visitor."

Horton reared upright out of the sleeping bag. He rubbed his sleep-smeared eyes to be sure of what he saw. A women stood off a pace or two, close beside the fire. She wore a pair of yellow shorts and white boots that reached halfway to her knees. She had on nothing else. A deep red rose was tatooed on one naked breast. She stood tall and had a willowy look about her. Strapped about her waist was a belt that supported a weird sort of handgun. A knapsack was slung across one shoulder.

"She came walking up the path," said Nicodemus.

The sun was not up yet, but the first dawn light had come. There was a wet, wispy, soft quality to the morning.

"You came up the path," said Horton, speaking fuzzily, still only half-awake. "Does that mean you came through the tunnel?"

She clapped her hands in pleasure. "How wonderful," she said. "You speak the elder tongue as well. How delightful to find the two of you. I studied your speech, but until now have never had a chance to use it. As I suspected, I realize now that the pronunciation we were taught had lost something through the years. I was astonished, and gratified as well, when the robot spoke it, but I could not hope that I'd find others . . .''

"It's passing strange, this thing she says," said Nicodemus. "Carnivore speaks the same tongue, and he learned it from Shakespeare."

"Shakespeare," said the woman. "Shakespeare was an ancient . . ."

Nicodemus jerked a thumb upward toward the skull. "Meet Shakespeare," he said, "or what is left of him."

She looked in the direction of his thumb. She clapped her hands again. "How charmingly barbaric!"

"Yes, isn't it?" said Horton.

Her face was thin to the point of boniness, but it was of an aristocratic cast. Her silver hair was skinned back from her face into a little topknot on the nape of her neck. The skinning back of the hair served to emphasize the boniness of her face. Her eyes were piercing blue and her lips were thin, with no color in them and without a trace of smile. Even when she had clapped her hands in joy, there had not been a smile. Horton found himself wondering if a smile was possible for her.

"You travel in strange company," she said to Horton.

Horton looked around. Carnivore was emerging from the doorway. He looked like an unmade bed. He stretched, thrusting his arms far above his head. He yawned, his fangs gleaming in full splendor.

"I'll get breakfast," said Nicodemus. "Are you hungry, ma'am?"

"Ravenous," she said.

"Meat we have," said Carnivore, "although not freshly killed. I make haste to welcome you to our small encampment. I am Carnivore."

"But a carnivore is a thing," she objected. "A classification. It is not a name."

"He is a carnivore and proud of it," said Horton. "That's what he calls himself."

"Shakespeare name me it," said Carnivore. "I hold another name, but it is not important."

"My name is Elayne," she said, "and I am glad to meet you."

"My name is Horton," said Horton. "Carter Horton. You may call me either one or both."

He crawled out of the sleeping bag and got to his feet.

"Carnivore said 'meat,' " she said. "Could he be talking about flesh?"

"That's what he means," said Horton.

Carnivore thumped his chest. "Meat is good for you," he said. "It gives you blood and bone. It tones up the muscles."

She shuddered delicately. "Meat is all you have?"

"We could manage something else," said Horton. "Food that we packed in. Dehydrated, mostly. Not the best to taste."

"Oh, the hell with it," she said. "I'll eat meat with you. It is only prejudice that has kept me from it all these years."

Nicodemus, who had gone into the Shakespeare house, now came out of it. He held a knife in one hand and a slab of meat in the other. He cut off a large chunk of the meat and handed it to Carnivore. Carnivore squatted on his heels and began tearing at the meat, blood running down his muzzle.

Horton saw the look of horror on her face. "We'll cook ours," he said. He walked over to a pile of firewood and sat down upon it, patting a place beside him. "Join me," he said. "Nicodemus will do the cooking. It will take a while." He said to Nicodemus,

"You'd better cook hers well. I'll take mine rare."

"I'll start hers first," said Nicodemus.

Hesitantly, she came over to the woodpile and sat down next to Horton.

"This," she said, "is the strangest situation I have ever encountered. A man and his robot talking the elder tongue. A carnivore who talks it as well, and a human skull nailed above a doorway. The two of you must be from one of the backwoods planets."

"No," said Horton. "We come straight from Earth."

"But that can't be," she said. "No one now is straight from Earth. And I doubt that even there they speak the elder tongue."

"But we are. We left Earth in the year . . ."

"No one has left Earth for more than a thousand years," she said. "Earth now has no base for far traveling. Look, how fast were you traveling?"

"At near light-speed. With a few stops here and there."

"And you? You were, perhaps, in sleep?"

"Of course, I was in sleep."

"At near the speed of light," she said, "there is no way to calculate. I know there were early calculations, mathematical calculations, but they were, at best, rough approximations, and the human race did not travel at the speed of light for a sufficient length of time to arrive at any true determination of the time dilation effect. Only a few interstellar ships traveling at the speed of light or less were sent out, and fewer of them returned. Before they did return, there were better systems for far traveling and, in the meantime, Old Earth had stumbled into a catastrophic economic collapse and a war situation—not a single, all-engulfing war, but many mean little wars—and in the process,

Earth's civilization was virtually destroyed. Old Earth is still there. Its remaining population may be climbing back again. No one seems to know; no one really cares; no one ever goes back to Old Earth. I can see you know nothing of all this.''

Horton shook his head. ''Nothing.''

''That means you were on one of the early light-ships.''

''One of the first,'' said Horton. ''In 2455. Or thereabouts. Maybe the first of the twenty-sixth century. I don't really know. We were put into cold-sleep; then there was a delay.''

''You were put on standby.''

''I guess that's what you'd call it.''

''We aren't absolutely sure,'' she said, ''but we think this is the year 4784. There is no certainty, really. Somehow history got all bollixed up. Human history, that is. There are a lot of other histories than Earth history. There was a time of confusion. There was an era of outpouring into space. Once there was a reasonable way to get into space, no one who could afford the going stayed on Earth. It required no great analytical ability to see what was happening to Earth. No one wanted to be caught in the crunch. For a great many years, there were not too many records. Those that did exist may have been erroneous; others were lost. As you might imagine, the human race passed through crisis after crisis. Not only on Earth, but in space as well. Not all the colonies survived. Some survived, but later failed, for one reason or another, to establish contact with other colonies, so were considered lost. Some still are lost—either lost or dead. The people went out into space in all directions—most of them without any actual plans, hoping that in time they'd find a planet where they could settle. They went out not only into space, but into time as well, and no one understood time factors. We still don't. Under those conditions, it would be easy to gain a century or two or lose a century or two. So don't ask me to swear what year it is. And history. That is even worse. We don't have history; we have legend. Some of the legend probably is history, but we can't be sure which is history and which is not.''

"And you came here by tunnel?"

"Yes. I am a member of a team that is mapping the tunnels.''

Horton looked at Nicodemus, who was crouched beside the fire, watching the cooking steaks. "Did you tell her?" Horton asked.

"I never had a chance," said Nicodemus. "She never gave me a chance. She was so excited about me talking what she called the 'elder tongue.' ''

"Tell me what?" asked Elayne.

"The tunnel's closed. It's inoperative.''

"But it brought me here.''

"It brought you here. It won't take you back. It's out of order. It works only one way.''

"But that's impossible. There is a control panel.''

"I know about the control panel," Nicodemus told her. "I'm working on it. Trying to fix it.''

"And how are you doing?''

"Not too well," said Nicodemus.

"We are trapped," said Carnivore, "unless the goddamn tunnel can be fixed.''

"Maybe I can help," said Elayne.

"If you can," said Carnivore, "I implore you do your utmost. Hope I had that if tunnel not fixed, I could join ship with Horton and the robot, but I think it over and it does not seem so. This sleep you talk about, this freezing frightens me. Have no wish to be frozen.''

"We have worried about that," Horton told him. "Nicodemus knows about the freezing. He has a sleep-technician transmog. But he only knows how to freeze humans. You might be different—a different body chemistry. We have no way to determine your body chemistry."

"So that is out," said Carnivore. "So tunnel must be fixed."

Horton said to Elayne, "You don't seem too upset."

"Oh, I suppose I am," she said. "But my people do not rail against fate. We accept life as it comes. Good and bad. We know there will be each."

Carnivore, finished eating, reared up, scrubbing at his bloodied muzzle with his hands. "I go hunting now," he said. "Bring home fresh meat."

"Wait until we've eaten," suggested Horton, "and I'll go along with you."

"Best not," said Carnivore. "You scare the game away."

He started walking off, then turned around. "One thing you can do," he said. "You can throw old meat in pond. But hold your nose while doing."

"I'll manage it," said Horton.

"So good," said Carnivore, and went stalking off, eastward along the path to the abandoned settlement.

"How did you fall in with him?" asked Elayne. "And what, actually, is he?"

"He was waiting for us when we landed," said Horton. "We don't know what he is. He said that he was trapped here, along with Shakespeare . . ."

"Shakespeare, from his skull, is human."

"Yes, but we know little more of him than we do of Carnivore. Although we may be able to learn more. He carried a volume of the complete Shakespeare, and he filled the book with writing, scribbling on the margins and end papers. Every place where there was white space left."

"You have read some of this scribbling?"

"Some of it. There's a lot yet to read."

"The meat is done," said Nicodemus. "There is only the one plate and the one set of silver. You will not mind, Carter, if I give them to the lady?"

"Not at all," said Horton. "I am handy with my hands."

"Okay, then," said Nicodemus. "I'm off to the tunnel."

"As soon as I have eaten," said Elayne, "I'll drop by to see how you're getting on."

"I wish you would," said the robot. "I can't make head nor tail of it."

"It's fairly simple," said Elayne. "There are two panels, one smaller than the other. The small one controls the shield over the larger panel, the control panel."

"There's not two panels," said Nicodemus.

"There should be."

"Well, there's not. There is just the one with the force shield over it."

"That means, then," said Elayne, "that it's not a mere malfunction. Someone closed the tunnel."

"The thought had been in my mind," said Horton. "A closed world. But why should it be closed?"

"I hope," said Nicodemus, "that we don't find out." He picked up his tool kit and left.

"Why, this is tasty," exclaimed Elayne. She wiped grease off her lips. "My people do not eat flesh. Although we know of those who do and have despised them for it as a mark of barbarity."

"We are all barbarians here," said Horton, shortly.

"What was all that about cold-sleep for the Carnivore?"

"The Carnivore loathes this planet. He wants to get off it. That's why he wants so badly for the tunnel to be opened. If the tunnel can't be opened, he'd like to leave with us."

"Leave with you? Oh, yes, you have a ship. Or do you?"

"We do. Out on the plain."

"Wherever that is."

"Just a few miles from here."

"So you'll be leaving. May I ask where you'll be headed?"

"Damned if I know," said Horton. "That is Ship's department. Ship says we can't go back to Earth. We've been gone too long, it seems. Ship says we'd be obsolescent if we did go back. That they wouldn't want us back, that we'd embarrass them. And from what you tell me, I guess there's no point in going back."

"Ship," said Elayne. "You talk as if the ship's a person."

"Well, in a way, it is."

"That's ridiculous. I can understand how, over a long period of time, you'd develop a feeling of affection for it. Men have always personalized their machines and tools and weapons, but . . ."

"Damn it," Horton told her, "you don't understand. Ship really is a person. Three persons, actually. Three human brains . . ."

She reached out a greasy hand and grasped his arm. "Say that again," she said. "Say it very slowly."

"Three brains," said Horton. "Three brains from three different people. Tied in with the ship. The theory was . . ."

She let loose of his arm. "So it is true," she said. "It wasn't legend. There really were such ships."

"Hell, yes. There were a number of them. I don't know how many."

"I talked about legends earlier," she said. "How you couldn't tell the difference between legend and history. How you couldn't be sure. And this was one of the legends—ships that were part human, part machine."

"It was nothing wonderful," he told her. "Oh, yes, I suppose wonderful, at that. But it tied in with our kind of technology—a melding of the mechanical and biological. It was in the realm of the possible. In the technological climate of our day, it was acceptable."

"A legend come to life," she said.

"I feel a little funny being pegged a legend."

"Well, not really you," she said, "but the entire story. It seemed incredible to us, one of those kind of things you can't quite believe."

"Yet you said better ways were found."

"Different ways," she said. "Faster-than-light ships, based on new principles. But tell me about yourself. You're not the only human on the ship, of course. They would not have sent out a ship with just one man aboard."

"There were three others, but they died. An accident, I'm told."

"Told? You didn't know about it?"

"I was in cold-sleep," he said.

"In that case, if we can't get the tunnel fixed, there is room aboard."

"For you," Horton said. "For Carnivore, as well, I suppose, if we faced the choice of taking him or leaving him behind. I don't mind telling you, however, that we don't feel quite easy with him. And there is the problem of his body chemistry."

"I don't know," she said. "If there were nothing else that could be done, I suppose I'd rather leave with you than to stay here forever. It does not seem a charming planet."

"I have that feeling, too," said Horton.

"But it would mean giving up my work. You must be wondering why I came through the tunnel."

"I've not had the time to ask. You said mapping. After all, it's your concern."

She laughed. "Nothing secretive about it. Nothing mysterious. A team of us are mapping the tunnels—or, rather, trying to."

"But Carnivore told us they are random."

"That's because he knows nothing of them. A lot of uninformed creatures probably use them, and, of course, for them they're random. The robot said there was only one box here?"

"That is right," said Horton. "A single oblong box. It looked like a control panel. With some sort of cover over it. Nicodemus thought the cover might be a force shield."

"Ordinarily there are two," she said. "To select your destination, you activate the first box. It requires placing three fingers in three holes and depressing the activation triggers. That causes your so-called force field to disappear from the selection panel. You then depress the destination button. Take your fingers out of the first box and the protection shield reappears on the panel. To get at the selection panel, you must activate the first box. After you have selected your destination, you go through the tunnel."

"But how do you know where you are going? Are

there symbols on the panel that tell you which button you should push?''

''That's the trick,'' she said. ''There are no destination symbols, and you don't know where you are going. I suppose the tunnel builders had some way of knowing where they were going. They may have had a system that could allow them to pick a correct destination, but, if so, we have failed to find it.''

''Then you are pushing buttons in the dark.''

''The idea,'' she said, ''is that while there are many tunnels and many destinations for each tunnel, neither the tunnels nor the destinations can be infinite. If you travel for a sufficient length of time, one of the tunnels is bound to bring you back to a place you've been before, and if you keep precise record of the button you pushed on each panel of each tunnel that you traveled and if enough of you do this, each of you leaving a record-communication at each panel before you go through another tunnel, so that if one of your teammates should pass the same way . . . I explain it badly, but you can see how, after many trials and errors, in a few instances tunnel and panel relationships can be worked out.''

Horton looked doubtful. ''The odds sound long to me. Have you ever come back, as yet, to any place you've been?''

''Not as yet,'' she said.

''How many of you are there? On the team, I mean.''

''I'm not sure. They keep adding members all the time. Recruiting them and adding them. It's a sort of patriotic thing to do. Insofar, of course, as any of us are patriotic. The word doesn't mean, I'm sure, what it did at one time.''

''How do you get your information back to base? To

headquarters? To wherever you are supposed to deliver it? That is, if you get any information.''

"You don't seem to understand," she said. "Some of us—perhaps many of us—never will get back, with or without information. We knew, when we took on the work, that we were expendable.''

"You don't sound as if you really care.''

"Oh, we care, all right. At least I do. But the work is important. Can't you see how important? It's an honor to be allowed to search. Not everyone can go. There are requirements that each of us must meet before we are accepted.''

"Like not giving a damn if you ever get back home again.''

"Not that," Elayne said, "but a sense of self-worth that is sufficiently strong to maintain you anywhere, no matter what sort of situation you may get yourself into. Not having to be home to be yourself. Sufficient to one's self. Not dependent upon any specific environment or relationship. Do you understand?''

"I think I catch the edge of it.''

"If we can work out a map of the tunnels, if we can establish the relationship of the various tunnels, then they can be used intelligently. Not just going blind in them as we must go now.''

"But Carnivore used them. And so did Shakespeare. You said you have to pick a destination, even if you don't know what that destination may be.''

"They can be used without destination selection. You can, with the exception of the tunnel on this planet, simply walk into them and go where the tunnel takes you. Under these conditions, the tunnels are truly random. Our guess is that if no destination is chosen, there is a calculated randomness, some sort of preset randomness. No three users—perhaps no hundred users—using the tunnels in this manner, will ever arrive at the same destination. We think it was a calculated means to discourage use of the tunnels by unauthorized persons.''

''And the builders of the tunnels?''

Elayne shook her head. ''No one knows. Who they were or where they came from or how the tunnels are constructed. No hint of the underlying principles. Some people think that somewhere in the galaxy the builders still live on and that portions of the tunnels still may be in use. What we have here may be only abandoned sections of the tunnel systems, a part of an ancient transportation system for which there is now no need. Like an abandoned road that is no longer used because it leads to places no one now wants to go to, places where all purpose of going has long since disappeared.''

''There are no indications of what kind of creatures the builders were?''

''A few,'' she said. ''We know they must have had hands of sorts. Hands with at least three fingers, or some sort of manipulatory organs with the equivalent of at least three fingers. They had to have that many to work the panels.''

''Nothing else?''

''Here and there,'' she said, ''I have found representations. Paintings, carvings, etchings. In old buildings, on walls, on pottery. The representations are of many different life-forms, but seemingly one particular life-form is always there.''

''Wait a minute,'' said Horton. He rose from the woodpile and went into the Shakespeare building, coming back with the bottle he had found the day before. He handed it to her.

''Like this?'' he asked.

She rotated the bottle slowly, then stopped and placed a finger on it. "This is the one," she said.

Her finger rested on the creature that stood inside the canister. "This one is poorly executed," she said. "And done at a different angle. In other representations, you can see more of the body, more details. These things sticking from its head . . ."

"They look like the antennae the Earth people of an ancient day used to pick up signals for their TV sets," said Horton. "Or it might represent a crown."

"They are antennae," said Elayne. "Biological antennae, I am sure. Perhaps sense organs of some sort. The head here looks to be a blob. All I've ever seen were blobs. No eyes, no ears, no mouth, no nose. Perhaps they have no need of these. The antennae may give them all the sensory input of which they have any need. Their heads may be no more than blobs, a thing to anchor the antennae. And the tail. You can't tell here, but the tail is bushy. The rest of the body, or what I could make of it in the other representations I have seen, is always vague as to detail—a sort of generalized body. We can't be sure they really look like this, of course. The whole thing may be no more than symbolic."

"The art execution is poor," said Horton. "Crude and primitive. Wouldn't you think that the people who could construct the tunnels could draw better pictures of themselves?"

"I've thought of that, too," Elayne said. "Maybe it's not they who draw the pictures. Maybe they have no sense of art at all. Maybe the art is done by other peoples, inferior people, perhaps. They may not draw from actual knowledge, but from myth. Perhaps the myth of the tunnel builders survives throughout a good part of the galaxy, shared in common by many different people, many different racial memories persisting through the ages.''

16

THE stench of the pond was horrifying, but as Horton approached it seemed to lessen. The first faint whiff of it had been worse than down here near the water's edge. Perhaps, he told himself, it smelled worse when it began to break up and dissipate. Here, where it lay heavy, the foulness of it was suppressed and masked by its other components, the nonstench components that went to make it up.

The pond, he saw, was somewhat larger than it had appeared when he first had seen it from the ruined settlement. It lay placid, without a ripple on it. The shoreline was clean; no underbrush or reeds or any other kind of vegetation encroaching on it. Except for occasional small runlets of sand brought down off the hillside by runoff water, the shore was granite. The pond apparently lay in a hollowed bowl in the underlying rock. And, as the shore was clean, so was the water. There was no scum upon it as might be expected in a body of stagnant water. Apparently no vegetation, perhaps no life of any sort, could exist within the pond. But despite its cleanliness, it was not clear. It seemed to hold within itself a dark murkiness. It was neither blue nor green—it was almost black.

Horton stood on the rocky shore, with the remnant of meat clutched in his hand. There was about the pond, about the bowl in which it lay, a sort of somberness that verged on melancholy, if not on actual fear. It was a depressing place, he told himself, but not entirely without its fascination. It was the kind of place where a man could crouch and think morbid thoughts—morbid and romantic. A painter, perhaps, could use it as a model to paint a canvas of a lonely tarn, capturing within his composition a sense of lonely lostness and divorcement from reality.

We all are lost, Shakespeare had written in that long paragraph at the end of *Pericles.* He had written only in an allegorical sense, but here, less than a mile from where he had written the paragraph, writing in the flaring of the homemade candle, was that lostness of which he had written. He had written well, that strange human from some other world, thought Horton, for it seemed now that everyone was lost. Certainly Ship and Nicodemus and himself were lost in the vastness of no-return, and from what Elayne had said, back there by the fire, the rest of humanity as well. Perhaps the only ones that were not were those people, that handful of people, who still remained on Earth. Poor as Earth might be this day, Earth still was home to them.

Although, come to think of it, Elayne and the other searchers of the tunnels might not be lost in the same sense that all the others were. Lost, perhaps, in the sense that they never knew where they might be going, or what kind of planet they would find, but definitely not lost in the sense that they ever needed to know exactly where they were—self-sufficient to the point that they had no need of other humans, no need of familiarity, strange people who had outgrown the need of home. And was that, he asked himself, the way to defeat the sense of lostness—to no longer need a home?

He walked close to the water's edge and hurled the meat far out. It landed with a splash and disappeared immediately, as if the pond had accepted it, reaching out and taking it, sucking it down into itself. Concentric ripples ran out from the center of the splash, but did not reach the shore. The ripples were suppressed. They ran for a ways and then were flattened out and disappeared, the pond returning to its calm serenity, to the black flatness of itself. As if, Horton told himself, it valued its serenity and did not tolerate disturbances.

And now, he thought, it was time to leave. He'd done what he had come to do, and it was time to leave. But he did not leave; he stayed. As if there were something there that told him not to leave, as if, for some reason, he should linger for a while, as a man may overstay his time at the bedside of a dying friend, wanting to leave, uncomfortable in the face of oncoming death, but still staying because of a feeling that it would be the negation of an old friendship if one were to leave too soon.

He stood and gazed about him. To the left loomed the ridge where the abandoned settlement was located. From where he stood, however, there was no sign of the settlement. The houses were hidden by the trees. Straight ahead lay what seemed to be a swamp and to the right a conical hill—a mound—that he had not noticed until now and which apparently did not stand out with distinctness from the settlement ridge.

It rose, he judged, a couple of hundred feet above the level of the pond. Symmetrical, it seemed a perfect cone, tapering to a jagged point. It had something of the appearance of a volcanic cinder cone, but he knew that it was not. Aside from the fact that it was apparent it could not be a cone, he could not pin down his immediate rejection of it as volcanic. Lone trees grew here and there upon it, but otherwise it was bare of vegetation except for the grasslike growth that covered it. Looking at it, he crinkled his brow in puzzlement. There was, he told himself, no geologic factor he had observed or could immediately bring to mind that would explain a formation of that sort.

He returned his attention to the pond, remembering what Carnivore had said—that it was not really water, that it was more like soup, too thick and heavy to be water.

Walking down to the edge of it, he squatted and carefully reached out a finger to test the fluid. The surface seemed to resist slightly, as if it might have a fairly tough surface tension. His finger did not plunge into it. Instead, under slight pressure, the surface became indented beneath his fingertip. He applied more pressure, and the finger broke through. Plunging in his hand, he rotated his wrist so that his cupped palm was uppermost. Lifting his hand slowly, he saw that he had a handful of fluid. It lay quietly in his curved palm, not seeping through his imperfectly closed fingers as water would have. It seemed to be in one piece. For the love of Christ, he thought, a piece of water!

Although by now he knew it wasn't water. Strange, he thought, that Shakespeare had known no more than it was soupy. Although perhaps he did. There was a lot of writing in the book, and he'd read only a few paragraphs of it. Like soup, Carnivore had said, but this bore no resemblance to soup. It was warmer than Horton had thought it would be, and heavier, although that was a matter of judgment and to be certain, the fluid would have to be weighed and there was no way he could weigh it. It was slippery to the touch. Like mercury, although it wasn't mercury; he was sure of that. He turned his wrist and allowed the fluid to run out. When it was gone, his palm was dry. The liquid was not wet.

Unbelievable, he told himself. A liquid warmer than water, heavier, cohesive, not wet. Perhaps Nicodemus had a transmog—no, the hell with that. Nicodemus had a job to do and once he'd got it done, they'd be getting out of here, off this planet, and on into space, to other planets probably, or perhaps to no planets at all. And if that should be the case, he'd stay in cold-sleep and not be revived. The thought did not seem to frighten him as much as it should have.

Now, for the first time, he admitted what had been at the back of his mind, more than likely, all the time. This planet was no good. Carnivore had said as much in his first words of greeting, that the planet was no good. Not frightening, not dangerous, not repulsive—just not worth a damn. Not the kind of place that a man would want to stay.

He tried to analyze the reasons for his thinking this, but there seemed to be no specific factors he could line up and count. It was just a hunch, an unconscious psychological reaction. Perhaps the trouble was that this planet was too much like the Earth—a sort of dowdy Earth. He had expected that an alien planet would be alien, not a pale, unsatisfactory copy of the Earth. More than likely, other planets were more satisfactorily alien. He'd have to ask Elayne, he told himself, for she would know. Strange, he thought, how she had come through the tunnel and walking up the path. Strange that on this planet two human lives would cross—no, not two, but three, for he was forgetting Shakespeare. Somehow fate had dipped down into its bag of tricks and had conjured up three humans, within a very limited space of time—so limited that they'd encounter one another or, in the case of Shakespeare, almost encounter one another—would, at least, all three of them, have impact on one another. Elayne was down at the tunnel now with Nicodemus, and in just a while he'd join them, but before he did, he probably should investigate the conical hill. Although how he'd investigate it or what his investigation would tell him, he had no idea. But somehow it seemed important that he have a look at it. More than likely he had the feeling, he told himself, because it seemed so out of place.

He rose from his squatting and walked slowly around the edge of the pond, heading for the hill. The sun, halfway up the eastern sky, was warm. The sky was pale blue, without a sign of cloud. He found himself wondering what the planet's weather pattern might be like. He'd ask Carnivore; Carnivore had been here long enough to know.

He rounded the pond and came to the foot of the hill. The ascent was so steep that he was forced to go almost on hands and knees, bending forward to claw at the grasslike ground cover to keep from falling back and to help himself along.

Halfway up he halted, breath rasping in his throat. He stretched at full length on the ground, clawing his hands into the soil to keep himself from sliding back. He twisted his head so he could see the pond. Now its surface was blue instead of black. The mirror blackness of it was reflecting the blueness of the sky. He was panting so hard with the effort of his climb that it seemed to him the hill was panting with him—or perhaps that some great heart inside of it was beating rhythmically.

Still half-winded, he got on hands and knees again and finally reached the top. There, on a small flat platform which crowned the hill, he looked down the other side and saw the hill truly was a cone. Around its entire circumference, the slope thrust upward at the selfsame angle as the one he'd climbed.

Sitting cross-legged, he stared out across the pond to where, on the opposite ridge, he could make out some of the masonry of the deserted settlement. He tried to trace the outline of the houses, but found it was impossible because of the heavy growth that broke up the lines. Slightly to his left stood the Shakespeare house. A thin trickle of smoke rose from the cooking fire. He could see no one around. Carnivore, more than likely, was not back from his hunting trip. Because of the dip of the ground, he could not see the tunnel.

As he sat, he pulled absentmindedly at the ground cover. Some of it came loose, clay clinging to the roots. *Clay,* he told himself, *that's funny.* What would clay be doing here? He got out a pocket knife and opening a blade, stabbed at the soil, digging a little pit. As far as he could dig, it was clay. What, he asked himself, if the entire hill was clay? A sort of monstrous frost boil, heaved up in a bygone day and remaining till this moment. He cleaned the blade and closed it, put the knife back into his pocket. It would be interesting, he thought, if he had the time, to untangle the geology of this place. But what difference did it make? It would take a lot of time and he didn't plan to stay that long.

Getting to his feet, he went carefully down the slope.

At the tunnel, he found Elayne and Nicodemus. She was sitting on a boulder watching Nicodemus work. He had a chisel and a hammer and was tapping out a line around the panel.

"You're back again," Elayne said to Horton. "What took you so long?"

"I did some exploring."

110

"In the city? Nicodemus told me about the city."

"Not in the city," said Horton, "and it isn't any city."

Nicodemus turned around, the hammer and chisel hanging in his hand. "I'm trying to chisel the panel out of the rock," he said. "Maybe if I can do that, I can get at its backside and work on it from there."

"What you'll do," said Horton, "is cut the wires."

"There wouldn't be any wires," said Elayne. "Nothing quite that crude."

"Maybe, too," said Nicodemus, "if I can free the panel, I may be able to pry the cover loose."

"The cover? You said it was a force field."

"I don't know what it is," said Nicodemus.

"I take it," said Horton, "that there was no second box. The one that triggered the cover."

"No," said Elayne, "and that means someone tampered with the setup. Someone who didn't want anyone to leave this planet."

"You mean the planet's closed?"

"I suppose that is it," she said. "I suppose there would have been some sign set up at the other tunnels warning against using the selector which would take anyone to this planet, but if so, the signs are long since gone, or maybe they are there and we don't know what to look for."

"Even if you found them," Nicodemus said, "you probably couldn't read them."

"That is right," said Elayne.

Carnivore came stalking along the path. "I am back with fresh new meat," he announced. "How are you doing here? Have you got it solved?"

"No," said Nicodemus, turning back to work.

"It takes you long," said Carnivore.

Nicodemus swung around again. "Get off my back!" he snapped. "You've been riding me ever since I started. You and your friend Shakespeare messed around for years without doing anything, and now you expect us to get it all worked out within an hour or two."

"But tools you have," wailed Carnivore. "Tools and training. Shakespeare, he had none of this, nor did I. It would seem, with tools and training . . ."

"Carnivore," said Horton, "we never told you we could do anything. Nicodemus said he'd try. You have no guarantee. Stop acting as if we're breaking a promise that we made you. There never was a promise."

"Better, perhaps," said Carnivore, "that we attempt some magic. Magic put together. My magic, your magic and her magic." He pointed at Elayne.

"Magic wouldn't work," said Nicodemus, shortly. "If there is such a thing as magic."

"Oh, there's magic, all right," said Carnivore. "That is not in question." He appealed to Elayne. "Would you not say so?"

"I have seen magic," she said, "or what was reputed to be magic. Some of it appeared to work. Not every time, of course."

"Happenstance," said Nicodemus.

"No, more than happenstance," she said.

"Why don't we all just clear out," said Horton, "and give Nicodemus a chance to do what he is doing. Unless," he said to Nicodemus, "you think you need some help."

"I don't," said Nicodemus.

"Let's go and see the city," Elayne suggested. "I'm dying to see it."

"We'll stop at the camp and pick up a flashlight,"

Horton said. He asked Nicodemus, "We have a flash-light, haven't we?"

"Yes," said Nicodemus. "You'll find it in the pack."

"You're going along with us?" Horton asked Carnivore.

"If you please, no," said Carnivore. "The city is a nervous place for me. I'll stay right here. I'll cheer the robot on."

"You'll keep your mouth shut," said Nicodemus. "You'll not breathe on me. You'll offer no advice."

"I'll act," said a humble Carnivore, "as if I were not here."

17

Committees had been her life, the grande dame admitted to herself, *and there had been a time when she had thought of this present matter as a committee action. Just another committee,* she had told herself, *trying to fight down the fear of what she had agreed to, trying to put it in commonplace and (to her) understandable terms so that it would present no place for fear to lodge. Although,* she remembered, *the fear of it had been outweighed by another fear. And why was it,* she asked herself, *that fear must be the motive? At the time, of course, except in certain secret moments, she had not admitted to the fear. She had told herself, and led others to believe, that she had acted out of pure unselfishness, that she had no other thought than the good of humankind. She was believed, or thought she was believed, because such a motive and her action fitted in so neatly with what she had been doing all her life. She was known for good deeds and a deep compassion for all suffering humanity, and it was easy to suppose that her devotion to the welfare of the people of the Earth was simply carrying over into this final sacrifice.*

Although, so far as she could recall, she had never thought of it as a sacrifice. She had been quite willing, she remembered, *to let others think so, at times had even encouraged such belief. For it seemed a very noble act to sacrifice oneself, and she wanted to be remembered for her noble acts, this final one the greatest of them all. Nobility and honor, she thought; those had been what she prized the most. But not, she was forced to agree, a quiet nobility and a silent honor, for if that had been the case she'd have not been noticed. That, for her, would have been unthinkable, for she needed notice and acclaim. Chairwoman, president, past president, national representative, secretary, treasurer—all of these and more—organization piled upon organization, until she had no time to think, with every moment occupied, always on the go.*

No time to think? she asked herself. Was that the reason behind all her frantic effort? Not the honor and the glory, but so she wouldn't have to think? So she wouldn't have to think of the ruined marriages, of the men who turned away, of the emptiness she felt as the years went on?

That was why she was here, she knew. Because she had been a failure—because she had failed not only others, but herself as well, and in the end had recognized herself as a woman who sought frantically for something she had missed, missing it, perhaps, because she did not recognize the value of it until it was too late.

And, in view of this, she knew, this present venture had turned out all right, although there had been many times when she had doubted it.

There has never been a time when I doubted it, said the scientist. *I was always sure.*

You peeked, said the grande dame, bitterly. *You peeked into my thoughts. Is there no privacy at all? One's own personal thoughts should be private. It is bad manners, peeking.*

We are one, said the scientist, *or we should be one. No longer three personalities, no longer one woman and two men. But a mind, one mind. Yet we stay apart. We stand apart more often than we are together. And in that way we have failed.*

We have not failed, said the monk. *We have only started. We have eternity and I am the one who can define eternity. All my life I lived for eternity, suspecting even as I lived for it that for me there would be no eternity. Not for me or for anyone. But now I know that I was wrong. We've found eternity, the three of us—or if not actual eternity, what could be eternity. We have changed and we will change and in the aeons before this materialistic ship has powdered into dust, we undoubtedly will become an eternal mind that will have no need of Ship nor even the biologic brains that now house our minds. We will become a single free agent that can roam forever across all infinity. But I think I told you I had a definition for eternity. Not a definition, really, but a pretty tale. The Church, you must understand, formulated through the years many pretty tales. This one has to do with a mile-high mountain and a bird. Every thousand years the bird, which for the purpose of the story, was extremely long-lived, would fly above the mountain and, in doing so, one of its wings would touch the mountain and wear away an infinitesimal segment of it. Each thousand years the bird did this and eventually wore the mountain, with the impact of its wing, down to a level plain. And this, you say, this wearing down of a mountain by the scraping of a bird's wing every thousand years, would be eternity. But you would be wrong. It would be no more than the beginning of eternity.*

It is a silly tale, said the scientist. *Eternity is not a term that lends itself to definition. It is a catch-all vagueness to which we cannot assign a value, any more than a value can be assigned to infinity.*

116

I liked the story, said the grande dame. *It has a pretty ring to it. It is the kind of simple story that I found so telling in the speeches that I made to many different groups in many different causes. But if you should ask me now to name those groups and the causes, I should find it difficult to list them. I wish, Sir Monk, that I had known your story. I would, I am sure, have found occasion to use it. It would have been most fetching. It would have brought the house down.*

The story is silly, said the scientist, *because long before your long-lived bird could have made even a tiny mark upon the mountain, the natural forces of erosion would have reduced it to a peneplain.*

You have the advantage over the other two of us, said the Monk disapprovingly. *You have a specific logic by which to guide your thoughts and interpret your experiences.*

The logic of mankind, said the scientist, *is a poor reed to lean upon. It is a logic dictated by observation and despite our many marvelous instruments, our observations were severely restricted. Now the three of us must formulate a new logic based upon our current observations. We will find, I am sure, much error in our earthly logic.*

I know but little of logic other than the logic I studied as a churchman, said the monk, *and that logic was more often based upon obscure intellectual gymnastics than on scientific observation.*

And I, said the grande dame, *operated on logic not at all, but upon certain techniques used to advance certain activities to which I had become committed, although I'm not sure that committed is the proper word to use. I have a hard time recalling now just how committed I might have been to the causes that I worked for. In all frankness, I think it was not so much the*

117

causes that motivated me as the opportunity which they gave me to hold and exercise certain positions of power. Thinking on it now, those positions of power which seemed so desirable and exhilarating, sink to nothing now. But I must, in all truth, have distinguished myself in the public mind, for how otherwise would I have been offered the honor bestowed upon the three of us when it was decided that one of us must be a woman. So I would suppose that heading numerous committees, serving upon many commissions, involved in sundry study groups upon subjects of which I knew next to nothing, and speaking to both small and large assemblies, must have seemed worthwhile. And after all this time, trying to make up my mind as to whether it is right for me to be here, I am glad they did. I am glad I'm here. If I were not, I would be nowhere, Sir Monk, for I don't think I was ever able to convince myself to believe in your construction of an immortal soul.

Not my construction, said the monk. *I did not believe, either, in everlasting life. I tried to make myself believe, because in my business it was basic that I should believe. And there was, as well, my fear of death, and I suppose, life as well.*

You accepted your post here with us, said the grande dame, *because of your fear of death, and I because of honor—because it was not in me to reject the honor and esteem. I felt I might be being conned into something I'd regret, but I had sought the limelight too long to be constitutionally capable of rejecting it. At the very least, I told myself, it was a way of going out in a greater flare of publicity than I had ever dreamed.*

And now, said the scientist, *it seems all right to you? You are satisfied your acceptance was correct?*

I am satisfied, she said. *I am even beginning to*

forget, which I find to be a blessing. There was Ronny and Doug and Alphonse . . .

Who were they? asked the monk.

The men I was married to. They and a couple of others whose names I can't recall. I don't mind telling you, although there was a time I would have, that I was something of a bitch. A rather queenly bitch, perhaps, but still a dirty bitch.

It seems to me, said the scientist, *that we are working out as it was intended. Taking somewhat longer, more than likely, than had been intended. But in another thousand years, perhaps, we may be able to become what we were meant to be. We are being honest with ourselves and with one another, and I imagine that must be a part of it. We cannot entirely slough off our humanity in so short a time. The human race spent two million years or so in developing that humanity and it's not something that can be peeled off as one would take off his clothes.*

And you, Sir Scientist?

Me?

Yes, what about yourself? The other two of us are finally honest. What about yourself?

Me? I've never thought of it. There's never been a doubt. Any scientist, especially an astronomer like myself, would have sold his soul to go. Come to think of it, figuratively, I may have sold my soul. I connived to be named to this conglomerate of intellectuality, or whatever you may call it. I connived to be named. I would have fought for it. I implored certain friends, most privately and discreetly, to second my nomination. I would have done anything at all. I did not think of my selection as an honor. I did not act as did the two of you, from fear, and yet, in a way, I may have. I was growing old, you know, and I was beginning to get that frantic feeling that little time was left, that the sands were running out. Yes, come to think of it, there may have been some fear, a subconscious fear. But, basically, it was the feeling that I could not afford to go down into the final dark with so much still to do. Not that what I observe now or what I deduce now will have any earthly impact, for I am no longer part of Earth.

But, in the final reckoning, I don't think that ever mattered. My work was not for Earth nor for my fellow-men, but for myself—for my own personal satisfaction and gratification. I did not look for plaudits. Unlike you, dear lady, I hid myself away. I shunned publicity. I gave no interviews and I wrote no books. Papers, certainly, to share my findings with my fellow workers, but nothing for the man in the street to read. I think, if you summed it up, that I am, or was, an extremely selfish man. I cared for no one but myself. I now am glad to tell you that my position with the two of you I find very comfortable. As if we were old friends, although we were never friends before, nor perhaps are any of the three of us really friends to the other two in the classical definition of friendship. But if we can get along, I think that under the circumstances, we can call that friendship.

What a crew we turn out to be, said the monk. *A selfish scientist, a glory-hunting woman, and a monk who was afraid.*

Was?

I'm afraid no longer. There is nothing that can touch me or either one of you. We have got it made.

We still have a way to go, said the scientist. *Here there is no place nor time for gloating. Humble, humble, humble.*

I've been humble all my earthly life, said the monk. *I'm through with being humble.*

18

"THERE is something wrong," said Elayne. "Something out of place. No, maybe that's not it. But there is a somethingness that we haven't found. There is a situation waiting here—perhaps not for us, but waiting."

She was tensed, almost rigid, and into Horton's mind came the remembrance of that old setter with which, at times, he had hunted quail. A sense of expectancy, a knowing and a not-quite-knowing, a standing on tiptoe with acute awareness.

He stayed, waiting, and finally, with a seeming effort, she relaxed.

Elayne looked at him with begging eyes, begging to be believed. "Don't laugh at me," she said. "I know there's something here—something most unusual. I don't know what it is."

"I'm not laughing at you," he told her. "I'll take your word for it. But how . . ."

"I don't know," she said. "Once, in a situation such as this, I would have distrusted myself. But not any longer. It has happened before, many times before. Almost like a certain knowing. Like a warning."

"You think it might be dangerous."

"There is no way to know," she said. "Just that sense of somethingness."

"We've found nothing so far," he said, and that was true enough. In the three buildings they had explored, there had been nothing but the dust, the rotting furniture, the ceramics, and the glass. To an archaeologist, there might have been significance, Horton told himself, but to the two of them, there had been simply oldness—a musty, dusty, repetitive oldness that was at once futile and depressive. At some time in the distant past intelligent beings had lived here, but there was, to his untrained eyes, no indication of their purpose here.

"I've often thought about it," she said. "Wondered about it. For I'm not the only one who has it. There are others. A new ability, an acquired instinct—there is no way of telling. When men went into space and landed on other planets, they were forced to adapt to—what would you call it?—the unlikely, perhaps. They had to develop new survival techniques, new habits of thinking, new insights and senses. Maybe that's what we have, a new kind of sense, a new awareness. The pioneers of Earth, when they pushed out into unknown areas, developed something of the sort. Primitive man had it, perhaps, as well. But back on old settled and civilized Earth, there came a time when there was no longer any need of it and it was lost. In a civilized environment there were few surprises. One knew fairly well what he might expect. But when he went out to the stars, he found a new need of this old awareness."

"Don't look at me," said Horton. "I'm one of those people from what you call civilized Earth."

"Was it civilized?"

"To answer that, you must define the term. What is civilized?"

"I wouldn't know," she said. "I have never seen a completely civilized world—not in the sense that Earth was civilized. Or I don't think I have. These days you

122

can't be sure. You and I, Carter Horton, come from different ages. There may be times when the only proper course will be for each of us to be patient with the other."

"You sound as if you've seen a lot of worlds."

"I have," she said. "On this mapping job. You reach a place, stay a day or two—well, maybe more than that, but never very long. Only long enough to make some observations and jot down some notes, to get an impression of what kind of world it is. So you'll be able to recognize it, you see, if you come back to it again. For it's important to know if the tunnel system ever brings you back to a place you've been before. Some places you'd like to stay awhile. Once in a great while, you find a really pleasant place. But there are few of these. Mostly you are glad to leave."

"Tell me one thing," Horton said. "I've been wondering about it. You are on this mapping expedition. That is what you call it. It sounds to me more like a wild-goose chase. Your chances can't be more than one in a million and yet . . ."

"I told you there are others."

"But even if there were a million of you, there'd be only one of you who has any chance of returning to a world that has been visited before. And just one of you finding their way back would be a waste of time. There'd have to be a number of you who succeeded before there could be any statistical probability the tunnels could be mapped, or even started to be mapped."

She stared coldly at him. "Back there where you came from, you, of course, had heard of faith."

"Certainly I have heard of faith. Faith in one's self, faith in one's country, faith in one's religion. What has that got to do with it?"

"Faith is often all that one possesses."

"Faith," he said, "is thinking something's possible when you're quite sure it's not."

"Why so cynical?" she asked. "Why so short of vision? Why so materialistic?"

"I'm not cynical," he said. "I just take the odds into some account. And we were not short of vision. We were the ones, remember, who first went to the stars and we were able to go, to persuade ourselves to go, because of the materialism you seem so much to scorn."

"That is true," she agreed, "but that's not what I am talking about. Earth was one thing; the stars are another. When you get out among the stars, the values change, the viewpoints shift. There's an ancient phrase—it's a different ball game—can you tell me what that phrase means?"

"I suppose it alludes to some sort of sports event."

"You mean those silly exercises that once were held on Earth?"

"You don't hold them any more? No sports events at all?"

"There is too much to do, too much to learn. We no longer need to seek artificial amusement. We haven't got the time, and even if we had, no one would be interested."

Elayne pointed at a building almost engulfed by brush and trees. "I think that's the one," she said.

"The one?"

"The one where the strangeness is. The something-ness that I have been talking about."

"Should we go and see?"

"I'm not entirely sure," she said. "To tell you the truth, I'm a little frightened. By what we might find, you know."

"You have no idea? You say you can sense this somethingness. Does your perception extend far enough to give you at least some hint?"

Elayne shook her head. "Only that it's strange. Something out of the ordinary. Perhaps frightening, although I feel no actual fright. Just a tugging at my mind, a fear of the unusual, of the unsuspected. Just this terrible sense of strangeness."

"It's going to be tough getting there," he said. "That growth is fairly dense. I could go back to camp and get a machete. I think that we brought one along."

"No need," she said. She unholstered the weapon on her belt.

"This will burn a path," she said. It was larger than it had looked when holstered, needle-nosed and a bit cumbersome.

He eyed it. "A laser?"

"I suppose so. I don't know. Not a weapon only, but a tool. It's standard on my home planet. Everyone carries one of them. You can adjust it, see . . ." She showed him the dial set into the grip. "A narrow cutting edge, a fan effect, whatever you may want. But why do you ask? You carry one as well."

"Different," said Horton. "A fairly crude weapon, but effective if you know how to handle it. It throws a projectile. A bullet. Forty-five caliber. A weapon, not a tool."

Elayne crinkled her brow. "I have heard of the principle," she said. "A very ancient concept."

"Perhaps," siad Horton, "but up to the time I left the Earth, the best we had. In the hands of a man who knows its operation, it is precise and very deadly. High velocity, tremendous stopping power. Powder-powered—nitrate, I think, maybe cordite. I'm not up on the chemistry."

"But powder—no compound—could last the many years that you were on the ship. It would break down with time."

Horton gave her a startled look, surprised at her knowledge. "I hadn't thought of that," he said. "But it's true. The matter converter, of course . . ."

"You have a matter converter?"

"That's what Nicodemus tells me. I haven't actually seen it. I have never seen one, to tell you the truth. There was no such thing as a matter converter when we went into cold-sleep. It was developed later."

"Another legend," she said. "A lost art . . ."

"Not at all," said Horton. "Technology."

She shrugged. "Whatever it is—lost. We have no matter converter. As I said, another legend."

"Well," asked Horton, "are we going to see what this something of yours is, or do we . . ."

"We'll go and see," she said. "I'll set it at the lowest power."

She leveled the contraption, and a pale blue haze leaped out from it. The underbrush puffed with an eerie whisper, and dust floated in the air.

"Careful," he cautioned.

"Don't worry," she said sharply. "I know how to use it."

It was evident she did. She cut a neat and narrow path, detouring around a tree. "No use of burning it. It would be a waste."

"You still feel it?" Horton asked. "The strangeness. Can you figure what it is?"

"It still is there," she said, "but I have no more idea what it is than I ever had."

She holstered the gun and, shining the light ahead of him, Horton led the way into the building.

The place was dark and dusty. Pieces of crumbling

furniture stood along the walls. A small animal squeaked in sudden terror and raced across the room, a blur of motion in the darkness.

"A mouse," said Horton.

Elayne said, unruffled, "Probably not a mouse. Mice belong on Earth, or so say the old nursery rhymes. There's that old one, hickory dickory dock, the mouse ran up the clock."

"Then the nursery rhymes survived?"

"Some of them," she said. "I suspect not all of them."

A closed door confronted them, and Horton put out his hand and pushed against it. The door collapsed and fell into a pile across the threshhold.

He lifted the torch and shone the light into the room beyond. The room flared back at them, a glare of golden light thrown back into their faces. They staggered back a step or two and Horton lowered the flash. Cautiously he raised it again and this time, through the flare of the reflected light, they saw what it was that had given rise to the reflection. In the center of the room, almost filling it, stood a cube.

Horton lowered the flash to cut down on the reflection and moving slowly, stepped into the room.

The light from the flash, no longer reflected by the cube, seemed to be absorbed by it, sucked in and spread out throughout its interior so that it seemed the cube was lighted.

A creature lay suspended in the light. A creature— that was the only description that would come to mind. It was huge, almost filling the cube, its body extending beyond their line of vision. For a moment, there was a sense of mass, but not just any kind of mass. There was a sense of life in it, a certain flow of line that said instinctively it was a living mass. What seemed to be a head was hunched down low against what may have been its chest. And the body—or was it a body? A body covered by an intricate filigree of etching. Like armor, Horton thought—an expensive example of the goldsmith's art.

Beside him, Elayne gasped with wonder. "It's beautiful," she said.

Horton felt frozen, half with wonder, half with fear. "It has a head," he said. "The damn thing is alive."

"It hasn't moved," she told him. "And it would have moved. At the first touch of light, it would have moved."

"It's asleep," said Horton.

"I don't think it's asleep," she said.

"It has to be alive," he said. "You sensed it. This has to be the strangeness that you sensed. You still have no idea what it is?"

"None at all," she said. "Nothing that I've ever heard about. No legends. No elder stories. Nothing at all. And so beautiful. Horrible, but beautiful. All those fine, intricate designs. It is something it is wearing— no, I see now it is not something it is wearing. The etchings are on scales."

Horton tried to trace the outline of the body, but each time he tried, he failed. He'd start out all right and trace it for a ways, then the outline would be gone, fading and dissolved in the golden haze that lingered in the cube, lost in the convoluted intricacies of the form itself.

He took a step forward for a closer look and was stopped—stopped by nothing. There was nothing there to stop him; it was as if he had run into a wall he could neither see nor feel. No, not a wall, he thought. His mind scurried frantically for some sort of simile that would express what had happened. But there seemed no simile, for the thing that stopped him was a nothing-ness. He lifted his free hand and felt in front of him. The hand found nothing, but the hand was stopped. No physical sensation, nothing he could feel or sense. It was, he thought, as if he had encountered the end of reality, as if he'd reached a place where there was nowhere to go. As if someone had drawn a line and said the world ends here, there is nothing that extends beyond this line. No matter what you see, or think you see, there is nothing there. But if that were true, he thought, there was something very wrong, for he could see beyond reality.

"There is nothing there," said Elayne, "but there must be something there. We can see the cube and creature."

Horton stepped back a pace and, in that moment, the goldenness of the cube seemed to flood out and enfold the two of them, making them a part of the creature and the cube. In that golden haze, the world seemed to go away and for the moment they stood alone, divorced from time and space.

Elayne stood close to him and looking down, he saw the rose tattooed on her breast. He reached out a hand and touched it.

"Beautiful," he said.

"Thank you, sir," she said.

"You do not mind that I noticed it?"

She shook her head. "I had been beginning to feel disappointed that you hadn't noticed it. You must have known that it was there to direct attention. The rose is intended as a focal point."

19

NICODEMUS said, "Take a look at this."

Horton bent to stare at the faint line the robot had chiseled in the stone around the perimeter of the panel.

"What do you mean?" he asked. "I see nothing wrong. Except that it seems you haven't made much progress."

"That is exactly what is wrong," said Nicodemus. "I have been getting nowhere. The chisel chips the stone for a depth of a few millimeters; then the stone gets hard. As if it were a metal with a small portion of its surface reduced to rust."

"But it isn't metal."

"No, it's stone, all right. I tried other parts of the rock face." He gestured toward the wall of stone, indicating scratches on it. "It's the same on the entire face. Weathering seems to be at work, but underneath the weathering, the stone is incredibly hard. As if the molecules were bonded more tightly than they should be naturally."

"Where is Carnivore?" asked Elayne. "He might know something of this."

"I doubt it very much," said Horton.

"I sent him packing," said Nicodemus. "I told him to get the hell out. He was breathing down my neck and cheering me on . . ."

"He is so terribly anxious to get off this planet," said Elayne.

"Who wouldn't be?" asked Horton.

"I feel so sorry for him," said Elayne. "You're sure there is no way to put him on the ship—if all else fails, I mean."

"I don't see how," said Horton. "We could try cold-sleep, of course, but it would more than likely kill him. What do you think, Nicodemus?"

"Cold-sleep is tailor-made for humans," said the robot. "How it would work with another species, I have no idea. I would suspect not too well, perhaps not at all. First of all, the anesthetic that shocks the cells into momentary suspension until the cold can take effect. Almost foolproof for humans because it is designed for humans. To work with some other form of life, there might have to be a change. The change might be small and rather subtle, I imagine. And I'm not equipped to change it."

"You mean he'd be dead even before he had a chance of freezing?"

"I would suspect that would be the case."

"But you can't just leave him here," said Elayne. "You can't go off and leave him."

"We could put him on board," said Horton.

"Not with me you can't," siad Nicodemus. "I'd kill him in the first week out. He's sandpaper on my nerves."

"Even if he escaped your homicidal tendencies," said Horton, "what would be the purpose? I don't know what Ship has in mind, but it could be centuries before we made planetfall again."

"You could stop and drop him off."

"You could," said Horton. "I could. Nicodemus could. But not Ship. Ship, I would suspect, takes a longer view. And what makes you think we'd find

131

another planet that he could survive on—a dozen years from now, a hundred years from now? Ship spent a thousand years in space before we found this one. You must remember that Ship is an under-light-speed vessel.''

"You are right," said Elayne. "I keep forgetting. During the time of the depression, when the humans fled from Earth, they went out in all directions.''

"Using faster-than-light.''

"No, not faster-than-light. Time-jump ships. Don't ask me how they worked. But you get the idea . . .''

"A glimmer," Horton said.

"And even so," she said, "they traveled many light-years to find terrestrial planets. Some disappeared—into vast distances, into time, out of this universe, there is no way to know. They've not been heard of since.''

"So you see," said Horton, "how impossible this matter of Carnivore becomes.''

"Perhaps we still can solve the tunnel problem. That is what Carnivore really wants. That is what I want.''

"I'm out of all approaches," said Nicodemus. "I have no new ideas. We are not dealing with a simple situation of someone simply closing a world. They went to a lot of work to keep it closed. The hardness of this rock isn't natural. No rock could be that hard. Someone made it hard. They recognized that someone might try to tamper with the panel and took steps against it.''

"There must be something here," said Horton. "Some reason for blocking the tunnel off. A treasure, perhaps.''

"Not a treasure," said Elayne. "They'd have taken a treasure with them. A danger, more than likely.''

"Someone who hid something here for safekeeping.''

132

"I don't think so," said Nicodemus. "Someday they'd want to recover it. They could reach it, of course, but how would they get it out?"

"They could come by ship," said Horton.

"That would be unlikely," said Elayne. "The better answer is they'd know how to bypass the block."

"You think there's a way to do it, then?"

"I'm inclined to think there might be, but that doesn't mean that we can find it."

"Then, again," said Nicodemus, "it may be a simple matter of blocking the tunnel so that something that is here cannot get out. Penning it in from the rest of the tunnel planets."

"But if that's the case," asked Horton, "what could it be? Would you think our creature in the cube?"

"That might be it," she said. "Imprisoned not only in the cube, but restricted to the planet. A second defense against it if it ever was able to escape the cube. Although it is hard, somehow, to think so. It is such a pretty thing."

"It could be pretty and still be dangerous."

"What's this cube creature?" asked Nicodemus. "I've not heard of it."

"Elayne and I found it in a building in the city. Some sort of thing enclosed in a cube."

"Alive?"

"We can't be certain, but I think it is. I had the feeling that it is. Elayne was able to sense it."

"And the cube? What is the cube made of?"

"A strange material," said Elayne, "if it is a material. It stops you, but you can't feel it. It's as if it weren't there."

Nicodemus began to pick up the tools scattered on the flat rock floor of the path.

"You're giving up," said Horton.

"I might as well. There's no more I can do. No tool I have will touch the stone. I can't lift off the panel's protective covering, be it force field or something else. I'm done until someone else comes up with a good idea."

"Perhaps if we had a look through Shakespeare's book, we'd come up with something new," said Horton.

"Shakespeare never came close," said Nicodemus. "The best that he could do was kick the tunnel and do a lot of cussing."

"I didn't mean we'd find any worthwhile ideas," said Horton. "At the best, an observation, the implications of which slipped past Shakespeare."

Nicodemus was doubtful. "Maybe so," he said. "But we can't do much reading with Carnivore around. He'll want to know what Shakespeare wrote, and some of the things that Shakespeare wrote were not too complimentary to his old pal."

"But Carnivore's not here," Elayne pointed out. "Did he say where he was going when you chased him off?"

"He said a walkabout. He mumbled something about magic. I gained the impression, none too clearly, that he wanted to collect certain magic stuff—leaves, roots, barks."

"He spoke of magic earlier," said Horton. "Some idea that we could combine our magics."

Elayne asked, "Have you any magics?"

"No," Horton said, "we haven't."

"Then you must not sneer at those who have."

"You mean you believe in magic?"

Elayne crinkled her brow. "I'm not sure," she said, "but I have seen a magic work, or seem to work."

Nicodemus finished with his toolbox and closed it.

"Let's get up to the house and see about that book," he said.

20

"THIS Shakespeare of yours," said Elayne, "seems to have been a philosopher, but a rather shaky one. Not at all well grounded."

"He was a lonely and an ill and frightened man," said Horton. "He wrote whatever came into his head, without examining the logic or the fitness of it. He was writing for himself. Never for a moment did he think anyone else would ever read what he was scribbling. If he had thought so, he probably would have been more circumspect in what he wrote."

"At least he was honest about it," she said. "Listen to this:

Time has a certain smell. This may be no more than a conceit of mine, but I am sure it has. Old time would be sour and musty and new time, at the beginning of creation, must have been sweet and heady and exuberant. I wonder if, as events proceed toward their unknowable end, we may not become polluted with the acrid scent of ancient time, in the same manner and to the same end as olden Earth was polluted by the spew of factory chimneys and the foulness of toxic gases. Does the death of the universe lie in time pollution, in the thickening of old time smell until no life can exist upon any of the bodies that make up the cosmos, perhaps eroding the very matter of the universe itself into a foul corruption? Will this corruption so clog the physical processes operative in the universe that they will cease to function and chaos will result? And if this should be the case, what would chaos bring? Not necessarily the end of the universe since chaos in itself is a negation of all physics and all chemistry, perhaps allowing for new and unimaginable combinations which would violate all previous conceptions, giving rise to a disorderliness and an imprecision which would make possible certain events that science now tells us are unthinkable.

"And he goes on:

This may have been the situation—I was first inclined to say a time and that would have been a contradiction in terms—when, before the universe came into being, there was neither time nor space and, as well, no referrents for that great mass of somethingness waiting to explode so our universe could come into existence. It is impossible, of course, for the human mind to imagine a situation where there'd have been neither time nor space except as each potentially existed in that cosmic egg, itself a mystery that is impossible for one to visualize. And yet, intellectually, one does know a situation such as this did exist if our scientific thinking is correct. Still, the thought occurs—if there were neither time nor space, in what sort of medium did the cosmic egg exist?

"Provocative," said Nicodemus, "but still it gives us no information, nothing that we need to know. The man writes as if he were living in a vacuum. He could write that sort of drivel anywhere at all. Only occasionally does he mention this planet, with parenthetical dirty digs at the Carnivore.''

''He was trying to forget this planet,'' said Horton, ''trying to retire within himself so that he could disregard it. He was, in effect, attempting to create a pseudo-world that would give him something other than this planet.''

''For some reason,'' said Elayne, ''he was concerned about pollution. Here is something else he wrote about it:

The emergence of intelligence, I am convinced, tends to unbalance the ecology. In other words, intelligence is the great polluter. It is not until a creature begins to manage its environment that nature is thrown into disorder. Until that occurs, there is a system of checks and balances operating in a logical and understandable manner. Intelligence destroys and modifies the checks and balances even as it tries very diligently to leave them as they were. There is no such thing as an intelligence living in harmony with the biosphere. It may think and boast it is doing so, but its mentality gives it an advantage, and the compulsion is always there to employ this advantage to its selfish benefit. Thus, while intelligence may be an outstanding survival factor, the factor is short-term, and intelligence turns out instead to be the great destroyer.

She flipped the pages, eyeing the entries briefly. ''It's so much fun reading the elder tongue,'' she said. ''I was not sure I could.''

"Shakespeare's penmanship was not of the best," said Horton.

"Still good enough to read," she said, "once you get the hang of it. Here's something strange. He's writing about the god-hour. That's a strange expression."

"It's real enough," said Horton. "At least here it's real. I should have told you of it. It is something that reaches out and grabs you and lays you absolutely open. Except for Nicodemus. Nicodemus barely reacts to it. It seems to originate elsewhere than this planet. Carnivore said that Shakespeare thought it came from some point far in space. What does he say about it?"

"Apparently he was writing about it after a long experience with it," she said. "Here is what he writes:"

I feel that I may finally have come to terms with this phenomenon that I have termed, for lack of a better description, the god-hour. Carnivore, poor soul, still resents and fears it, and I suppose I fear it, too, although by this time, having lived with it for many years and learning that there is no way one may hide from it or insulate oneself from it, I have reached some acceptance of it as something from which there is no escape, but likewise as something that can, for a time, take a man outside himself and expose him to the universe, although, truth to tell, if it were optional, one would hesitate to thus have himself exposed too often.

The trouble is, of course, that one sees and experiences too much, most of which—nay, all of which—he does not understand and is left, after the event, holding onto only the ragged edge of it, with the horrifying wonderment as to whether a human mentality is equipped and capable of understanding more than a modicum of that to which he has been exposed. I have wondered at times if it could be a deliberate teaching mechanism, but if it is, it is an over-education, a throwing of massive scholarly texts at a stupid student who has not been grounded in the basic fundamentals of what he is being taught and thus incapable of even feebly grasping at the principles which are necessary for even a shadowy understanding.

I have wondered, I say, but wonder is about as far as this particular thought has ever gotten. As time went on, I became more and more of the opinion that in the god-hour I was experiencing something that was not intended for me at all, nor for any human—that the god-hour, whatever it may be, emanates from some sort of entity that is entirely unaware that such a thing as a human may exist, which might be caught up in cosmic laughter were it to learn that such a thing as I am did exist. I am, I had become convinced, simply caught up in the shotgun effect of it, sprayed by some stray pellets that were aimed at bigger game.

But no sooner had I become convinced of this than I was made acutely aware that the source of the god-hour somehow had at least marginally become aware of me and had somehow managed to dig deep into my memory or my psyche, for at times, instead of being laid open to the cosmos, I was laid open to myself, laid open to the past, and for a period of unknown duration lived over again, with certain distortions, events of the past which almost invariably were distasteful in the extreme, moments snatched out of the muck of my mind, where they had lain deeply buried, where in shame and regret I would have wished to keep them buried, but now dug up and spread out before me while I squirm in embarrassment and indignity at the sight of them, forced to live again certain parts of my life that I had hid away, not only from the ken of others, but of myself as well. And even worse than that, certain fantasies that in unguarded moments I had dreamed in my secret soul and been horrified when I found what I had been dreaming. And these, too, are dragged squealing from my subconscious and paraded in an unpitying light before me. I don't know which is worse, the opening to the universe, or the unlocking of the secrets of myself.

So I became aware that somehow the god-hour had become aware of me—perhaps not actually of me as a person, but as some fleck of obscene and disgusting matter and had flicked at me in irritation that such a thing as I should be there, not taking the time to really do me any harm, not squashing me as I might squash an insect, but simply brushing me, or trying to brush me, to one side. And I took some courage, strangely, from this, for if the god-hour is only marginally aware of me, then I told myself I stand in no actual danger from it. And if it pays so slight attention to me, then surely it must be seeking bigger game than I and the terrifying part of this is that it seemed to me that this bigger game must be here, upon this planet. Not on this planet only, but on this particular segment of the planet—it must be very near to us.

I have wracked my brains in an effort to imagine what it might be and if it still is here. Was the god-hour intended for the people who inhabited the now-deserted city, and if this should be the case, how is it that the agency which is responsible for the god-hour does not know that they are gone? The more I think of it, the more convinced I become that the people of the city did not supply the target, that the god-hour still is aimed at something that is still here. I look for what it may be, and I have no idea. I am haunted by the feeling that I look upon the target day after day and do not recognize it. It is frustrating and an eerie sensation to be thinking this. One feels out of touch and stupid and, at times, more than a little frightened. If a man can be so out of touch with reality, so blind to actuality, so insensitive to his surroundings, then the human race, in all truth, is more unfit and feeble than we have sometimes thought.

As she came to the end of what Shakespeare had written, Elayne raised her head from the page and looked at Horton. "Do you agree?" she asked. "Did you have some of the same reactions?"

"I've gone through it only twice," Horton told her. "The sum total of my reactions so far is a vast bewilderment."

"Shakespeare says it is inescapable. He says there is no way to hide from it."

"Carnivore hides from it," said Nicodemus. "He gets under cover. He says it's not so bad when you are under cover."

"You'll know in a few hours more," said Horton. "I have a hunch it's easier if you don't try to fight it. There is no way it can be described. You must experience it to know."

Elayne laughed, a little nervously. "I can hardly wait," she said.

21

CARNIVORE came clumping in an hour before sunset. Nicodemus had cut steaks and was squatting, broiling them. He motioned at a huge chunk of meat he had laid upon a bed of leaves pulled off a nearby tree.

"That's for you," he said. "I picked a choicest cut."

"Nourishment," said Carnivore, "is a thing I stand in need of. I thank you from my gut."

He picked up the chunk of meat in both his hands and hunkered down in front of the woodpile on which the other two were seated. He lifted it to his face and bit vigorously into it. Blood spouted on his whiskers.

Chomping vigorously, he looked up at his two companions.

"I do not bother you, I hope," he said, "with my unseemly eating. I hunger greatly. Perhaps I should have waited."

"Not at all," said Elayne. "Go ahead and eat. Ours will be ready in a little time." She gazed in sick fascination at his bloody chops, the blood running down his tentacles.

"You like good red meat?" he asked.

"I'll get used to it," she said.

"You don't really have to," said Horton. "Nicodemus could find you something else."

She shook her head. "When you travel world to

world, you find many customs that are strange to you. Some that may even be a shock to your prejudice. But, in my way of life, there can be no prejudice. Your mind must stay open and receptive—you must force it to stay open."

"And this is what you're doing by eating meat with us?"

"Well, it was to start with and I suppose it is still a little. But without half trying, I think I could develop a fondness for the flesh." She said to Nicodemus, "Could you make sure that mine is on the well-done side?"

"I already have," said Nicodemus. "I started yours well ahead of Carter's."

"I have been told many times by my old friend Shakespeare," said Carnivore, "that I am an unmitigated slob, with no manners worth the mentioning, and dripping, filthy habits. I am, to tell you truth, devastated at such evaluation, but I am too long in the tooth to change my way of life, and I would, on no account, become a mincing dandy. If I be a slob, I shall enjoy being one, for slobbishness is a comfortable situation in which to find oneself."

"You're a slob, all right," said Horton, "but if it makes you happy, pay us no attention."

"Thankful I am for your graciousness," said Carnivore, "and happy I do not have to change. Change is hard for me to do." He said to Nicodemus, "You have the tunnel nearly done?"

"Not only is it not nearly done," said Nicodemus, "but now I'm fairly sure it will not be done."

"You mean fix it you cannot?"

"That's exactly what I mean unless someone comes up with a bright idea."

"Oh, well," said Carnivore, "while hope forever

144

springs inside the gut, I am not surprised. I walked for long today with myself communing, and I told myself too much I should not expect. I say to myself that life has not been hard on me and many happinesses I've had, and that in view of this, I should not gag at some wrong events. And I sought within my mind alternatives. It seemed to me that magic might be a way to try. You say to me, Carter Horton, that you do not trust nor understand the magic. You and Shakespeare are the same. He make heavy fun of magic. He say it no damn good. Perhaps our newest compatriot may not think so strongly." He looked appealingly at Elayne.

She asked, "Have you tried your magic?"

"That I have," he told her, "but against Shakespeare's scornful hooting. The hooting, I tell myself, take the edge off it, reduce it down to nothing."

"I don't know about that," said Elayne, "but I'm sure it would do no good."

Carnivore nodded sagely, "Then I say to myself, if magic fails, if the robot fails, if all else fails, what am I to do? Remain upon this planet? Surely not, I say. Surely these new friends of mine will find a place for me when off this world they fly into deeper space."

"Now you're leaning on us," Nicodemus said. "Go ahead and bawl. Roll on the ground and kick your heels and scream. It won't do you any good. We can't put you in cold-sleep and . . ."

"At least," said Carnivore, "I am with friends. Until I die, I am with friends and away from here. I take little space. I huddle in one corner. I eat very little. I am not in the way. I will keep my mouth shut."

"That will be the day," said Nicodemus.

"It's up to Ship," said Horton. "I will talk with Ship about it. But I can hold out no hope."

"You comprehend," said Carnivore, "that I am a

warrior. There is but one way for a warrior to die, in the bloodiness of fighting. That is how I want to die. But that may not be the way of it with me. To fate, I bow my head. What I do not want is die here, with no one to see me die, to think poor Carnivore, he is gone, to crawl out my last days in the loathesome nothingness of this place passed by in time . . ."

"That's it," said Elayne, suddenly. "Time. That is what I should have thought of right at first."

Horton looked at her in astonishment. "Time? What are you talking about? What has time to do with it?"

"The cube," she said. "The cube we found in the city. With the creature in it. That cube is frozen time."

"Frozen time!" said Nicodemus. "Time can't be frozen. You freeze people and food and other things. Time you do not freeze."

"Arrested time," she said. "There are stories— legends—that it can be done. Time flows. It moves. Stop its flow and movement. No past, no future, just the present. An everlasting present. A present existing from the past and embedded in the future that now has become the present."

"You sound like the Shakespeare," grumbled Carnivore. "Always spouting foolishness. Always yak, yak, yak. Saying things with no sense in them. Just to hear his talk."

"No, it's not that at all," insisted Elayne. "I tell you the truth. There are stories on many planets that time can be manipulated, that there are ways to do it. No one can say who does it . . ."

"Perhaps the tunnel people."

"There never is a name. Just that it can be done."

"But why here? Why with the creature frozen into time?"

"Perhaps to wait," she said. "Perhaps so it will be

here when the need for it arises. Perhaps the ones who put the creature into time could not know when that need would come . . ."

"So it's waited through the centuries," said Horton, "with millennia still to wait . . ."

"But don't you see," she said. "Centuries or millennia, it would be all the same. Frozen as it is, it has no time experience. It exists and continues to exist within that frozen microsecond . . ."

The god-hour struck.

22

FOR a moment, Horton was spattered across the universe, with the same sickening sense of endlessness that he had felt before; then the spattering came together and the universe was narrowed, and all sense of strangeness ceased. There was coordinated time and space again, neatly tied together, and he knew where he was, except there seemed to be two of him, although the twoness of him seemed not inconvenient and even natural.

He crouched in the warm black loam between two rows of vegetables. Ahead of him, the two rows went on and on, two green lines with a strip of black between them. To the left and right, there were innumerable other parallel green lines with the black lines between them—although he had to imagine the black lines, for the greenness of the green lines merged together and on either side, there was only a dark green carpet.

Squatting on his heels, feeling the warmth of the soil against his bare feet, he looked back over his shoulder and behind him the green carpet ended, very far away, against the uplift of a structure that towered so high its top was lost in a white puffy cloud pegged against the blueness of the sky.

He reached out his little boy's hands and picked the

beans that hung heavily on the plants, using his left hand to pull the bushes apart so he could reach the pods entangled in the foliage, picking them with his right hand and dropping them into a half-filled basket sitting in the black loam strip just in front of him.

Now he saw what he had not seen before, that at regular intervals between rows, ahead of him other baskets waited, empty baskets waiting to be filled, placed there by rough calculation of when one basket would be filled and another needed. And back of him other baskets, already filled and waiting for the vehicle which later on would move along the rows to collect the baskets filled with beans.

Something else he had not realized before—that he was not alone in the field, but that there were many others with him, most of them children, although some were old men and women. Some of them were ahead of him, being faster, or perhaps less careful, pickers, others behind him.

Clouds flecked the sky, fleecy, lazy clouds, but at the moment none covered the sun and it shone down with a fierce warmth that he could feel striking through the thinness of his shirt. He crawled along the row, picking as he went, being conscientious in his work, leaving some of the smaller pods to mature for another day or two, picking all the others—with the sun upon his back, sweat starting in his armpits and running down his ribs, the softness and the warmth of the well-broken, cultivated soil pressing on his feet. His mind held in neutral, clinging to the present, neither moving back nor forth in time, content in the present moment, as if he were a simple organism which absorbed the warmth and in some strange way drew nourishment from the soil, as had the beans he picked.

But there was more than that. There was the boy, perhaps nine or ten, and there was, as well, the present Carter Horton, a seemingly invisible second person, who stood to one side, or was positioned somewhere else, who watched the boy he once had been, feeling and thinking and experiencing what he once had known, almost as if he were the boy. But knowing more than the boy knew, knowing what the boy could not even guess, aware of the years and events which lay between this expansive bean field and a time a thousand light-years into space. Knowing, as the boy could not know, that men and women in the great distant structure which rose at one end of the field, and in many other similar structures in the world, had recognized the seeds of another crisis-point and, even then, were planning its solution.

Strange, he thought, that even given a second chance, the human race still must come upon its crisis-points and realize at last that the only solution lay in other possible planets in other hypothetical solar systems, where men once more could make other starts, some of these starts failing, but some, perhaps, succeeding.

Less than five centuries before this morning in the bean patch, the Earth had faltered to a halt, not in war, but in worldwide economic collapse. With the profit and free-enterprise system finally buckling under the cracks which had begun to be apparent early in the twentieth century, with a large fraction of the world's more basic natural resources gone, with population soaring, with industry introducing more and more technological labor-saving devices, with food surpluses no longer stretching far enough to feed the people of the world—with all of these, famine, unemployment, inflation, and a lack of confidence in world leadership had resulted. Government had disappeared; industry, communications and trade had ground to a halt and, for a time, there had been anarchy and chaos.

Out of this anarchy had risen another way of life, put together, not by politicians and statesmen, but by economists and sociologists. But in a few hundred years, this new society had exhibited symptoms which had sent the scientists to their laboratories and engineers to their drafting boards to design the starships that would transplant the human race to space. The symptoms had not been misread, the second, the invisible Horton told himself, for on this very day (which day? this day or another day?) Elayne had told him of the final collapse of the way of life the economists and sociologists had carpentered so carefully.

Earth had been too sick, he thought, too debased, too exploited, too polluted by the errors of mankind to survive.

He felt the soil between his toes and the little whiff of breeze that came across the field to blow against his sweat-soaked, sun-warmed back. He dropped the handful of beans that he had picked into the basket and pushed it ahead of him, hunching along the row to reach other bushes in the seemingly never-ending row of bushes. The basket, he saw, was almost full. Just ahead of him was an empty basket.

He was getting tired. Glancing at the sun, he saw that it was still an hour or more till noon when the lunch wagon would come driving down the rows. A half hour for lunch, he thought, and then he'd be back at the picking until the sun went down. He stretched out the fingers of his right hand, flexing them to take away the cramp and tired. He saw that the fingers were stained green.

Tired and hot and beginning to get hungry and a long

day yet ahead, but he had to keep on picking, as hundreds of others were picking—the very young and the very old—doing jobs that they could do, leaving other more capable workers free to do other jobs. He squatted on his heels and stared out across the greenness. Not only beans, he thought, but many other crops in season, produce that when the time came must be harvested to feed the people of the tower.

To feed the people of the tower, thought Horton (the insubstantial, invisible Horton), to feed the tribe, the clan, the commune. My people. Our People. One for all and all for one. The tower built high, above the clouds, so that it would take little ground space, piling a city perpendicularly so that the land would be left to grow the food to feed the people of the piled-up city. People crowded into a tower because the tower, huge as it was, must be as small as possible.

Make do. Make last. Get along without. Grow and harvest food with stoop labor because there was little fuel. Eat carbohydrates because they took less energy to grow than protein. Build and manufacture for permanence and not for obsolescense; with the profit system swept away, obsolescence had become not only criminal, but ridiculous.

With industry gone, he thought, we grew our food, we took in one another's washing. We got along—we got along. We went back to tribal patterns, living in a monolith rather than a collection of rude huts. In time, we sneered at the olden times, at the profit system, at the work ethic, at private enterprise and all the time we sneered, there was a sickness in us—the sickness of humankind. No matter what we tried, he told himself, there was a sickness in us. Must it be that the human race cannot live in harmony with its environment? Must it, to survive, have new planets to rape each few millennia? Are we doomed to move like an invading swarm of locust across the galaxy, across the universe? Is the galaxy, the cosmos, doomed to us? Or will the day come when the universe will rise up in annoyance and slap us down—not in anger, but in annoyance? There is, he thought, a certain greatness in us, but a destructive and a selfish greatness. Earth lasted for a matter of two million years after our species first arose, but during most of those years, we were not effective as we now are effective—it took us a time to grow up to our full potential for destruction. But starting, as we are now, on other planets, how long would it take to introduce that deadly virus of mankind—how long will it take the disease to run its course?

The boy parted the bushes and was reaching out to pick the beans thus exposed. A worm which had been clinging to the leaves lost its footing and dropped off. Striking the ground, it rolled itself into a ball. Scarcely without thinking, scarcely pausing in his work, the boy shifted a foot, lifting it to come down on the worm, grinding it deep into the soil.

A gray mist came creeping to blot out the bean field, and the great monolithic building that loomed mile-high in the distance and there, hanging in the sky, surrounded by the misty fog that swept about it in streaming tendrils was the skull of Shakespeare, looking down at Horton—not leering down at him, not grinning down at him, but regarding him most companionably, as if the flesh might still exist, as if the barrier line of death did not exist at all.

Horton found himself speaking to the skull. "How now, old companion?" And that was strange, for Shakespeare had never been his companion save in the general companionship of humanity, the two of them belonging to that strange and awesome race of creatures which had proliferated on one planet and then, in desperation rather than adventurously, had gone storming out into the galaxy—going only God knew how far, for certainly, at this moment, no member of the race might know with any certainty how far the others may have gone.

"How now, old companion?" And that was strange as well, for Horton knew that it was not the manner in which he'd ordinarily speak—almost as if he were speaking in a sort of Mother Goose adaptation of the kind of speech the original Shakespeare had used to pen his plays. As if he were not the original Carter Horton, but, as well, another Mother Goose adaptation mouthing rote sentiments to some symbolism that he once had dreamed. He raged inwardly at himself for being what he was not; but try as he could, he could not find himself again. His psyche was so entangled with the boy who crushed a worm and with a dried-bone skull case that there was no way he could find the path back to his normal self.

"How now, old companion?" he asked. "You say we all are lost. But where lost? How lost? Why lost? Have you dug down to the basics of our lostness? Is it carried in our genes, or did something happen to us? Are we the only lost ones, or are there others like us? Is lostness an innate characteristic of intelligence?"

The skull said to him, clattering its bony jaws, "We are lost. That is all I said. I did not go digging into the philosophy of it. We are lost because we lost the Earth. We are lost because we do not know where we are. We are lost because we can't find the way back home. There now is no place for us. We walk strange roads in stranger lands and along the way, there is nothing that makes sense. Once we knew some answers because we knew the questions to be asked,

154

but now we can find no answers because we do not know the questions. When others in the galaxy reach out to make contact with us, we do not know what to say. We are, in such a situation, gibbering idiots who have not only lost our way, but our sense as well. Back there in your precious bean field, even at the age of ten, you had some sense of your purpose and where you might be going, but you do not have that same sense now.''

"No," said Horton, "I don't suppose I have."

"You're damned right you haven't. You want some answers, do you?''

"What kind of answers?''

"Any kind of answers. Any kind at all are better than no answers. Go and ask the Pond.''

"The Pond? What could the Pond tell me? It's just a glob of dirty water.''

"It's not water. You know it isn't water.''

"That's right. It isn't water. Do you know what it is?''

"No, I don't," said Shakespeare.

"Did you talk with it?''

"I never dared. Basically, I'm a coward.''

"You were afraid of the Pond?''

"Not that. Afraid of what it might tell me.''

"But you knew something about the Pond. You figured it could talk with you. And yet you never wrote about it.''

"How can you know?" asked Shakespeare. "You have not read everything I wrote. But you are right; I never wrote about it except to say it stank. And I never wrote about it because I did not want to think about it. It gave rise to great unease in me. It was more than just a pond. Even had it been no more than water, it would have been more than just a pond.''

"But why unease?" asked Horton. "Why did you feel that way about it?"

"Man prides himself upon his intellect," said Shakespeare. "He glorifies in his reason and his logic. But these are new things, very lately come by. Before that, he had something else. It was this something else that told me. Call it a gut feeling; call it intuition; call it any fancy name you wish. Our prehistoric ancestors had it, and it served them well. They knew, but could not tell you how they knew. They knew what to be afraid of and that, at the bottom of it, is what any species must have if it is to survive. What to be afraid of, what to walk around, what to leave alone. If you have that, you'll live; if you don't, you won't."

"Is this your spirit talking to me? Your shade? Your ghost?"

"First tell me this," said the skull, clattering its jaws with the two teeth missing. "First tell me what is life and what is death, and then I'll answer you about the spirit and the shade."

23

THE Shakespeare skull hung above the doorway, grinning down at them—and a moment before, Horton told himself, it had not been grinning. It had been talking with him as another man might talk. It had been strange, but it had not been horrible, and it had not grinned. Its two missing teeth had been no more than missing teeth, but now they had about them a macabre quality that was unsettling. Evening dusk had fallen, and the flicker of the fire reflecting off the polished bone made it seem that the jaws might still be moving and lent a blinking to the deep darkness of the sockets where once the eyes had been.

"Well," said Nicodemus, staring at the steaks, "this business of the god-hour has messed my cooking most atrociously. These slabs of meat are burned almost to a crisp."

"It's all right," said Horton. "I like my eating rare, but it doesn't matter that much."

Beside Horton, Elayne seemed to be emerging from a trance. "Why didn't you tell me?" she asked, accusingly. "Why didn't you let me in on what it would be like?"

"There is no way," said Carnivore. "How can you tell the shriveling of the gut . . ."

"What was it like?" asked Horton.

"Frightening," she said. "But wonderful as well. As if someone had taken you to some great cosmic mountaintop, with the universe all spread out before you—all the glory and the wonder, all the sadness. All the love and hate, all the compassion and not-caring. You stand there, frail and blown by the wind that sweeps the worlds and, at first, you are lonely and confused and you feel as if you are someplace you are not meant to be, but you remember then that you did not aspire to be there, but were somehow brought there and then it seems all right. You know what you are looking at, and it does not look anyway at all the way you would have imagined that it would—if, in fact, you ever had imagined that you'd see it, which you never did, of course. You stand and stare at it, at first with no comprehension and then, slowly, you begin to comprehend just a little, as if someone were telling you what it was all about. And, at last, you begin to understand, using truths you had not known existed, and you're about ready to say to yourself so that's the way it is and then, before you can say it to yourself, it all is gone. Just when you feel that you are ready to grasp some meaning of it, then it all is gone."

That was the way it was, thought Horton—or at least that was the way it had been. But this time, for him, it had been different, as Shakespeare had written; it could be different. And the logic of that difference, the reason for that difference?

"I timed it this time," said Nicodemus. "It ran slightly under a quarter of an hour. Did it seem that long?"

"Longer," said Elayne. "It seemed to last forever."

Nicodemus looked questioningly at Horton. "I don't know," said Horton. "I had no very clear impression of time."

The conversation with Shakespeare had not lasted too long, but when he tried to calculate, in memory, how long he had been in the bean field, he could not even make a guess.

"It was the same for you?" asked Elayne. "You saw much the same I did? This was what you could not describe to me?"

"This time it was different. I went back to my boyhood."

"And that was all?" asked Elayne. "Just back to your boyhood?"

"That was all," said Horton. He could not bring himself to tell of his conversation with the skull. It had an odd sound to it and more than likely, Carnivore would panic at the telling. It was better, he decided, to simply let it lie.

"The thing I want," said Carnivore, "is this god-hour to tell us how to fix the tunnel. You are quite sure," he said to Nicodemus, "that no farther you can go."

"I can't imagine what," said Nicodemus. "I tried to get the cover off the control, and that seems impossible. I tried to chisel out the control, and that rock is hard as steel. The chisel bounces off it. It's not just ordinary rock. In some way, it has been metamorphosed."

"Magic we could try. Among the four of us . . ."

"I know no magic," Nicodemus told him.

"Nor do I," said Horton.

"I know some," said Carnivore, "and perhaps m'lady."

"What kind of magic, Carnivore?"

"Root magic, herb magic, dancing magic."

"Those all are primitive," said Elayne. "They have but small effect."

"By the very nature of it, all magic is primitive,"

said Nicodemus. "It is the appeal of the ignorant to powers that are suspected, but of which no one is sure."

"Not necessarily so," said Elayne. "I know of peoples who have workable magic—magic you can count on. Based, I think, on mathematics."

"But not our kind of mathematics," said Horton.

"That is right. Not our kind of mathematics."

"But you don't know this magic," said Carnivore. "The mathematics you don't have."

"I'm sorry, Carnivore. I have no inkling of them."

"You put down my magic," howled Carnivore. "You, all of you, put me down most snottily. At my simple magic, of roots and leaves and barks, you sneer with quiet accomplishment. Then you tell me of other magic that might have a chance to work, that might open wide the tunnel, but you do not know this magic."

"Once again," Elayne told him, "I am very sorry. I wish, for your sake, I did have the magic. But we are here and it is somewhere else, and even if I could go in search of it, to find those who could manipulate it, I am not sure that I could interest them in such a project. For they, undoubtedly, would be very supercilious people and no easy folks to talk with."

"No one," said Carnivore, with feeling, "really gives a damn. You, all three of you, can go back to the ship . . ."

"We could go back to the tunnel in the morning," said Nicodemus, "and have another look at it. We might see something we have missed. After all, I spent all my time on the control panel, and no one paid attention to the tunnel itself. We might find something there."

"You'd do this?" asked Carnivore. "You'd really do it for good old Carnivore?"

"Yes," said Nicodemus. "For good old Carnivore."

And now, thought Horton, *this is the end of it. They'd go out tomorrow morning and inspect the tunnel once again. Finding nothing, there'd be no more they could do—although, come to think of it, that was wrongly phrased; up to the moment, they'd done exactly nothing. After several thousand years, if one took Elayne's dates at face value, they had finally reached a planet where a man could live, and then had gone rushing off on a rescue mission which had come to nothing. It was illogical for him to be thinking this, he told himself, but it was the truth. The only thing of value they had found had been the emeralds and, in their situation, the emeralds were not worth the picking off the ground. Although, perhaps, on second thought, they had found something that might be worth the time expended. But it was something, on the face of it, to which they could lay no claim. By all that was right and proper, Canivore must be the heir of Shakespeare, and this would mean that the Shakespeare volume must belong to him.*

He glanced up at the skull affixed above the door. *I would like that book,* he told the skull, speaking in his mind. *I'd like to settle down and read it, try to live the days of your exile, to judge the madness and the wisdom in you, finding, no doubt, more wisdom than madness, for even in madness there may, at times, be wisdom, try to correlate chronologically the paragraphs and snatches that you wrote so haphazardly, to find the kind of man you were and how you came to terms with loneliness and death.*

Did I really talk with you? he asked the skull. *Did you reach out beyond the death-dimension to establish contact with me, perhaps specifically to tell me about the Pond? Or was it simply a reaching out to anyone, any other intellectual blob, that was in a position to suspend a natural disbelief and to thus be able to talk with you? Ask the Pond, you said. And how do you ask the Pond? Do you walk up to the Pond and say, Shakespeare said I could talk with you—so go ahead and talk? And what do you really know about the Pond? Could there have been more than you wished to tell me, but did not have the time to do it? It is safe to ask you all this now, for you cannot answer. Although, it helps one to believe that he talked with you by now bombarding you with a flurry of questions that one knows will not be answered, not by a thing of weathering bone pegged above a doorway.*

You told Carnivore none of this, but then you'd not have told Carnivore; for in your madness, you must have feared him even more than you allowed your writing to reveal. You were a strange man, Shakespeare, and I'm sorry that I could not know you, but perhaps I know you now. Perhaps I know you better than I would have known you in the flesh. Perhaps even better than Carnivore could have known you, for I'm a human and Carnivore was not.

And Carnivore? Yes, what of Carnivore? For now it was at an end and someone must make some decision on what they were to do for Carnivore. Carnivore—the poor damn slob, the unlovable and disgusting, and yet something must be done for him. After raising up his hopes, they could not simply walk away and leave him here. Ship—he should have asked Ship about it, but he had been afraid to. He'd not even tried to contact Ship, for if he did, when he did, the matter of Carnivore

162

would come up and he knew the answer. It was an answer that he didn't want to hear, one that he couldn't bear to hear.

"That pond stinks hard tonight," said Carnivore. "There are times when it stinks more than others, and when the wind is right, there is no living with it."

As the words penetrated his consciousness, Horton again became aware of the others seated about the fire, with the Shakespeare skull no more than a splotch of whiteness hung above the door.

The stench was there, the foul rottenness of the Pond, and out beyond the circle of the campfire-light came a swishing sound. The others heard it and their heads turned to stare in the direction from which the sound had come. Listening hard for the sound to repeat itself, no one spoke.

The sound came again and now there was a sense of movement in the outer darkness, as if a part of the darkness had moved, not a movement one could see, but a sense of movement. A small part of the darkness took on a sheen, as if one small facet of the darkness had become a mirror and was reflecting back the firelight.

The sheen grew larger and there was now an unmistakable movement in the darkness—a sphere of deeper dark that was rolling closer, swishing as it came.

First there had been only a hint of it, then a sensing of it, and now, quite suddenly and unmistakably, it revealed itself—a sphere of darkness, two feet or so in diameter, that came rolling from the night into the circle of the firelight. The stench came with it—a deepening stench that seemed, however, as the sphere came closer, to lose some of its pungency.

Ten feet from the fire, it stopped and waited, a black ball that held within itself an oily gleam. It simply sat

163

there. It was motionless. There was no quiver, no pulsation, no sign that it had ever moved or was capable of movement.

"It's the Pond," said Nicodemus, speaking quietly as if he did not wish to disturb or frighten it. "It's from the Pond. A part of the Pond come visiting."

There was tension and fear within the group, but not, Horton told himself, an overriding fear—rather a shocked and wondering fear. Almost, he thought, as if the sphere was being very circumspect to hold down their fear.

"It's not water," said Horton. "I was there today. It is heavier than water. Like mercury, but it isn't mercury."

"Then a part of it could make itself into a ball," said Elayne.

"Alive the damn thing is," squeaked Carnivore. "It lies there, knowing of us, spying on us. Shakespeare say something wrong with Pond. He afraid of it. He go nowhere near it. Shakespeare be most accomplished coward. He say at times that in cowardliness lies a depth of wisdom."

"There is a lot going on," said Nicodemus, "that we don't understand. The blocked tunnel, the creature encased in time, and now this. I have a feeling that something is about to happen."

"How about it?" Horton asked the sphere. "Is there something that is about to happen? Have you come to tell us?"

The sphere made no sound. It did not stir. It simply sat and waited.

Nicodemus took a step toward it.

"Leave it alone," said Horton, sharply.

Nicodemus halted.

The silence held. There was nothing to be done,

nothing to be said. The Pond was here; the next move was up to it.

The sphere stirred, quivering, and then it was retreating, rolling back into the darkness until there was no sign of it, although long after it had disappeared, it seemed to Horton that he could still see it. It sloshed and rustled as it moved and this sound finally died out with distance and the stench, to which they had grown somewhat accustomed, began to clear away.

Nicodemus came back to the fire and squatted down beside it.

"What was that all about?" he asked.

"A look it wanted of us," wailed Carnivore. "It came to have a look."

"But why?" asked Elayne. "Why would it want to have a look at us?"

"Who can know what a Pond may want," said Nicodemus.

"There's one way to find out," said Horton. "I'll go and ask the Pond."

"That's the craziest thing I have ever heard," said Nicodemus. "This place must be getting to you."

"I don't think it's crazy," said Elayne. "The Pond came visiting. I'll go with you."

"No, you won't," said Horton. "I'm the only one to go. You all stay here. No one goes with me and no one follows. Is that understood?"

"Now, look, Carter," said Nicodemus, "you can't just go rushing off . . ."

"Let him go," growled Carnivore. "It is nice to know that all humans aren't like my cowardly friend there above the door."

He lurched to his feet and threw a rough, almost mocking salute to Horton. "Go, my warrior friend. Go to meet the foe."

24

HE got lost twice, missing turns in the path, but finally reached the pond, clambering down the steep incline above its edge, the light of the torch reflecting off the hard polish of its surface.

The night was deathly quiet. The Pond lay flat and dead. A scattering of unfamiliar stars dusted the sky. Looking behind him, Horton could see the glow of the campfire lighting up a tall treetop.

He planted his heels on the shelving stone that led down to the Pond and hunkered low.

"All right," he said, speaking both with tongue and mind, "let's have it."

He waited and it seemed to him there was a slight stirring in the Pond, a rippling that was not quite a ripple and from the farther shore came a whisper like wind blowing gently in a patch of reeds. He felt as well a stirring in his mind, a sense that there was something building in it.

He waited and now the thing was no longer in his brain, but by some shifting of certain coordinates of which he had no knowledge, aside from thinking that there must be coordinates involved, he seemed to become displaced. He was hanging, it seemed, as a disembodied being, in some unknown emptiness which contained a single object, a blue sphere that gleamed in the glare of sunlight that came over his left shoulder, or where his left shoulder should have been, for he could not be certain he even had a body.

The sphere was either moving toward him or he was falling toward it—which it was, he could not be certain. But, in any case, it was growing larger. As it grew, the blueness of its surface became mottled with ragged patches of whiteness, and he knew the sphere to be a planet with parts of its surface obscured by clouds which until now had been masked by the intense blueness of its surface.

Now there was no question he was falling through the atmosphere of the planet, although the fall seemed so controlled that he felt no apprehension. It was not like a fall, but rather a wafting downward, like a thistledown floating in the air. The sphere as such had disappeared, its disc become so large that it filled and overran his field of vision. Below him now lay the great plain of blueness with the brushed-in whiteness of the clouds. Clouds, but no other pattern, no sign of a continental mass.

He was moving faster now, plunging downward, but the illusion of thistledown still held. As he came closer to the surface, he could see that the blueness was ruffled—water set in motion by the raging wind that swept across it.

Not water, something said to him. Liquid, but not water. A world of liquid, a thalasso-planet, a liquid world with no continents nor islands.

Liquid?

"So that is it," he said, speaking with his mouth in his head in his body crouching on the shore of the Pond. "So that is where you came from. That is what you are."

And he was back again, a puff of thistledown hung

167

above a planet, watching, below him, a great upheaval in the ocean, with the liquid humping up and out, rounding and shaping itself into a sphere, perhaps many miles across, but, otherwise, quite like that other sphere that had come on a visit to the campfire. The sphere, he saw, was lifting, rising in the air, rising slowly at first, then gathering speed until it was coming at him like an outsize cannonball shot directly at him. It did not hit him, but it didn't miss him by too great a margin. His thistledown self was seized and buffeted by the turbulence of air disrupted by the passage of the liquid sphere. Far behind it, he could hear the long rumbling of the thunder as the split atmosphere came crashing back into the vacuum that had been created by the passage of the sphere.

Looking back, he saw that the planet was receding swiftly, plummeting backward into space. That was strange, he thought—that this should be happening to the planet. But, almost immediately, he realized it was not the planet to which it was happening, but to himself. He had been captured by the attraction of the massive liquid cannonball and, bouncing up and down, fluttered by its gravity, he was going along with it into the depths of space.

Nothing seemed to make any sense. He seemed to have lost all orientation. Except for the liquid cannonball and the distant stars, there were no reference points and even these reference points seemed to have but little meaning. He had, it seemed, lost all measurement of time and space appeared to have no yardstick quality and while he retained something of his personal identity, it had dimmed to only a flicker of identity. That's what happens, he told himself, complacently, when you haven't any body. A million light-years could be no more than a step away, and a million years no more than the ticking of a second. The one thing of which he was aware was the sound of space, which was like an ocean plunging over a waterfall a thousand miles in height—and another sound, a high singsong, a cricket noise almost too high for his auditory sense to catch, and that, he told himself, was the sighing of the heat lightning which flared just this side of infinity and the flaring of the lightning, he knew, was the signature of time.

Suddenly, while he looked away a moment, he became aware that the sphere he trailed through space had found a solar system and was streaking down through dense atmosphere to circle one of the planets. Even as he watched, the sphere bulged out on one side and humped up to form another smaller sphere, which fell away from it and began an orbit of the planet, while the larger parent sphere curved outward to plunge into space again. As it curved, it shook him loose and spun him out and he was free, tumbling toward the dark surface of the unknown planet. Fear dug deep claws into him and he opened his mouth to scream, astonished that he had a mouth to scream.

But before he could get the scream out, there was no need to scream, for he was back inside his body crouched beside the Pond.

His eyes were screwed tight shut and he opened them, with the feeling that he had to pry them open rather than merely open them. He could see fairly well despite the darkness of the night. The Pond lay placid in its rocky bowl, an unrippling mirror glittering with the light of the stars that hung in the sky above. To the right, the mound reared up, a conelike shadow in the darkness of the land, and, to the left, the ridge upon which the ruined city stood was a black beast crouching.

"So that is how it is," he said, speaking softly to the

Pond, no more than a whisper, as if it were a secret they must keep between themselves. "A colony from that liquid planet. One, perhaps, of many colonies. But why colonies? What does the planet derive from colonies? A living ocean that sends out small segments of itself, small buckets of itself, to seed other solar systems. And seeding them, what does it gain? What does it hope to gain?"

He quit his speaking and crouched in the midst of silence, a silence so profound that it was unnerving. A silence so deep and uncompromising that it seemed to him he could still hear the high singsong hiss of time.

"Speak to me," he pleaded. "Why don't you speak to me? You can show-and-tell; why can't you speak?"

For this was not enough, he told himself. Not enough to know what the Pond might be or how it had gotten there. This was a beginning only, a basic background fact, saying nothing of motive or hope or purpose and those three were important.

"Look," he said, still pleading, "you're one life and I'm another life. By our very natures we cannot harm one another, have no reason to wish harm for one another. So there is nothing for either of us to fear. Look, I'll put it this way—is there something that I can do for you? Is there something you want to do for me? Or lacking that, which well might be the case since we operate on such different planes, why don't we try to tell each about the other, get to know one another better. You must have some intelligence. Surely this seeding of the planets is more than just instinctive behavior, more than a plant broadcasting its seeds to take root in other soil, even as our coming here is more than a blind sowing of our cultural seed."

He sat, waiting, and again there was a stirring in his mind, as if something had entered it and was striving to form a message there, to draw a picture there. Slowly, by painful degrees, the picture grew and built, at first a shifting, then a blur, and, finally, hardening into a cartoonlike representation that changed and changed again and yet again, becoming clearer and more definitive with each change until it seemed that there were two of him—two hims squatting there beside the Pond. Except that one of him was not simply squatting there, but held in its hand a bottle—the very bottle he'd brought back from the city—and was stooping to dip the bottle into the liquid of the Pond. Fascinated, he watched—the both of him watched—as the neck of the bottle gurgled, sending up a spray of breaking bubbles as the liquid of the Pond, filling the bottle, forced out the air within it.

"All right," said the one of him. "All right and then what do I do?"

The picture changed and the other of him, carrying the bottle carefully, was walking up the ramp into the Ship, although Ship came off rather badly, for it was lopsided and distorted, as bad a representation of the Ship as the etchings on the bottle must have been bad representations of the creatures they were intended to depict.

The figure of his second self by now had entered the Ship and the ramp was rising and the Ship was lifting off the planet, heading into space.

"So you want to go along," said Horton. "For the love of God, is there anything on this planet that doesn't want to go with us? But so little of you, just a jugful of you."

This time the image in his mind formed swiftly—a diagram that showed that far-distant liquid planet and many other planets with globes of the liquid either heading for them or leaving them, with little drops

171

shaken off the spheres falling on the planets the parent spheres were seeding. The diagram changed, and lines were drawn from all the seeded planets and the liquid planet itself into a point in space where all the lines came together with a circle drawn around that point where the lines converged. The lines disappeared but the circle stayed and again the lines were swiftly drawn to converge with the circle.

"You mean—?" asked Horton and the same thing took place again.

"Inseparable?" asked Horton. "Are you saying there is only one of you? That there are not many of you, but only the one of you? That there's just one I? No we, but a single I? That you here before me is only an extension of one single life?"

The square of the diagram went white.

"You mean that's right?" asked Horton. "That's what you did mean?"

The diagram faded from his mind and in its place came a feeling of strange happiness, of satisfaction, of a problem solved. No word, no sign. Just the sense of being right, of having caught the meaning.

"But I talk with you," he said, "and you seem to understand. How come you understand?"

There was a squirming in his mind again, but this time no picture formed. There were flutterings and vague shapes and then it all was gone.

"So," he said, "there's no way you can tell me." But, perhaps, he thought, there was no need to tell him. He should know himself. He could talk with Ship, through the contraption, whatever it might be, that had been grafted on his brain, and perhaps here the same sort of principle was involved. He and Ship talked in words, but that was because they both knew the words.

172

They had a common medium of communication, but with Pond that medium did not exist. So Pond, grasping some meaning from the thoughts he'd formed inside his mind when he spoke—the thoughts that were brother to his words—had fallen back upon the most basic of all forms of communications, pictures. Pictures painted on a cave wall, etched on pottery, drawn on paper— pictures in the mind. The acting-out of thought processes.

I guess it doesn't matter, he told himself. Just so we can communicate. Just so ideas can cross the barrier between us. But it was so insane, he thought—a biologic construct of many different tissues talking to a mass of biologic liquid. And not only the few gallons of liquid lying in this rocky bowl, but the billions upon billions of gallons of liquid on that distant planet.

He stirred, shifting his position, the muscles of his legs cramped with squatting.

"But why?" he asked. "Why would you want to go with us? Surely not to plant another tiny colony—a bucket colony on some other planet that we may reach in time, perhaps centuries from now. Such a purpose makes no sense. You have far better ways to plant your colonies."

Swiftly the picture formed inside his mind—the liquid planet shimmering in its devastating blueness against the jet backdrop of space, and spearing out from it thin, jagged lines, many thin, jagged lines aimed at other planets. And even as he saw the lines snake out across the diagram, Horton seemed to know that the other planets at which the lines were aimed were those planets upon which the liquid planet had established colonies. Strangely, he told himself, those jagged lines bore some resemblance to the human-conventional sign for thunderbolts, realizing that Pond had borrowed from him certain conventionalities to implement its communication with him.

One of the many planets in the diagram zoomed toward him until it was larger than all the others and he saw that it was not a planet, but was Ship, still lopsided, but Ship undeniably, with one of the lightning bolts shattering against it. The lightning bolt bounced off Ship and came streaking straight toward him. He ducked instinctively, but was not quick enough and it struck him straight between the eyes. He seemed to shatter and was flung across the universe and was stripped naked and laid open. And as he spattered across the universe, a great peace came out of somewhere and settled softly on him. In that instant, for a flaring second, he saw and understood. Then it all was gone and he was back again, in his own body, on the rocky shelf beside the Pond.

The god-hour, he thought—it's unbelievable. Yet, as he thought more upon it, it gained belief and logic. The human body—all sophisticated, biologic bodies—had a nervous system that was, in effect, a communication network. Why, knowing this, should he balk at the thought of another communication network, operating across the light-years, to tie together the many scattered segments of another intelligence? A signal to remind each scattered colony that it still was a part and would remain a part of the organism, that it was, in fact, the organism.

A shotgun effect, he had earlier told himself—caught in the spray of pellets that had been aimed at something else. That something else, he now knew, was Pond. But if it had been only a shotgun effect, why should Pond now want to include him and Ship in that spray of god-hour pellets? Why did it want him to take on board a bucket of itself to provide a target that would include him and Ship in the god-hour? Or had he misunderstood?

"Have I misunderstood?" he asked the Pond and in answer, he felt again the scattering, the opening-out and the peace that came with it. Funny, he thought, he had not known the peace before, but only fright and befuddlement. The peace and understanding, although this time there had only been the peace and none of the understanding, and that was just as well, he thought, for even as he'd sensed it, he had gained no idea of the understanding, of what kind of understanding it might be, but simply the knowledge, the impression, that there was an understanding and that, in time, it might be grasped. To him, he realized, the understanding had been as befuddling as all the rest of it. Although not to everyone, he told himself; Elayne, for an instant, had seemed to grasp the understanding—grasping it in one instinctive instant, then losing it again.

Pond was offering him something—him and Ship— and it would be boorish and ungracious to see in what it offered anything but the wish of one intelligence to share with another something of its knowledge and its insight. As he had told Pond, there should be no conflict between two such dissimilar life-forms. By the very nature of their differences, there should be no competition nor antagonism between them. And yet, far in the back of his mind, he heard the tinny ringing of the alarm bells that were built into every human brain. That was wrong, he told himself, fiercely, that was unworthy; but the ringing of the bells went on and on. You do not make yourself vulnerable, chimed the bells, you do not expose your soul, you trust nothing until proven tests—proven many times—you can be triply certain that no harm will come.

Although, he told himself, the offering by Pond might not be totally selfless. There might be some part of humanity—some knowledge, some perspective or viewpoint, some ethical judgment, some historical evaluation—that Pond could use. Thinking this, he felt a surge of pride that there might be something human-kind could contribute to this unsuspected intelligence, giving some evidence that intelligent entities, no matter how dissimilar they might be, could find a common ground, or learn a common ground.

Apparently Pond was offering, for whatever reason, a gift which had great value in its scale of values—no gaudy trinket such as a greater, arrogant civilization might offer a barbarian. Shakespeare had written that the god-hour might be a teaching mechanism and it could be that, of course. But it could be, as well, he thought, a religion. Or simply no more than a recogni-tion signal, a clan call, a convention to remind Pond and all the other Ponds throughout the galaxy of the unity, the I-ness, of all of them with one another and their parent planet. A sign of brotherhood, perhaps—and if this were the case, then he, and through him, the human race, was being offered at least a provisional position in the brotherhood.

But it was more, he was certain, than a mere recogni-tion signal. On the third time it had come to him, he had not been triggered to the symbolic experience he had lived through the times before, but to a scene out of his own childhood and to a quite human fantasy in which he had talked with Shakespeare's clacking skull. Was that mere triggering or had it happened because the mechanism (the mechanism?) responsible for the god-hour had wormed its way into his mind and soul, in fact examining and probing and analyzing him as it, those first two times, had appeared to do. Something of the sort, he remembered, apparently had been experienced by Shakespeare.

"Is there something that you want?" he asked. "You do this for us—what can we do for you?"

He waited for the answer, but there was no answer. Pond lay dark and placid, with the starlight freckling its surface.

You do this for us, he'd said; what can we do for you? Making it sound as if what Pond had offered was something of great value, something that was needed. Was it? he asked himself. Was it something that was needed, that was even wanted? Was it not, perhaps, something they could do without, most happily without?

And was ashamed. First contact, he thought. Then knew he was wrong. First contact for him and Ship, but perhaps not first contact for Pond or the many other Ponds on many other planets. Nor first contact for many other humans. Since Ship had left the Earth, man had spread across the galaxy, and these splinters of humanity must have made many other first contacts with creatures strange and wonderful.

"Pond," he said. "I spoke to you. Why don't you answer, Pond?"

A tiny flutter stirred within his mind, a contented flutter, like the soft sighing of a puppy settling down to sleep.

"Pond!" he said.

There was no answer. The flutter was not repeated. And this was the end of it, the all of it? Perhaps Pond was tired. It struck him as ridiculous that such a thing as Pond was tired.

He rose to his feet, and his cramped leg muscles cried

relief. But rising to his feet, he did not move immediately, standing there and listening to the amazement that thundered through his brain.

He had been disappointed, he remembered, at his first glimpse of the planet, disappointed at its lack of alienness, thinking of it as no more than just a dowdy Earth. It was, he said, defending his first impression, dowdy enough, if it came to that.

Now that it was time to go, now that he'd been dismissed, he found a strange reluctance to leave. As if, having struck up a new friendship, he hated to say good-bye. The term was wrong, he knew; it was not a friendship. He sought for the right word for it. There was none that he could think of.

Could there, he wondered, ever be an actual friendship, a bone and blood friendship, between two intelligences so totally different. Could they ever find that common ground, that area of agreement, where they could say to one another: I agree with you—you may have approached the concept of a common humanity and a common philosophy from a different standpoint, but your conclusions coincide with mine.

It was unlikely, he told himself, in detail, but on the basis of broad principles, it might be possible.

"Good night, Pond," he said. "I am glad I finally met you. I hope it will go well with the both of us."

Slowly he climbed the rocky shore and set out down the path, using the flashlight to find his way.

As he rounded a bend, the light picked up a blur of whiteness. He shifted the light. It was Elayne.

"I came to meet you," she said.

He walked up to her. "It was a foolish thing to do," he told her. "You could have lost your way."

"I couldn't stay back there," she said. "I had to hunt

you out. I'm frightened. There is something about to happen."

"The sense of awareness once again?" he asked. "Like when we found the creature caught in time?"

She nodded. "I would suppose that's it. Just a feeling uncomfortable and on edge. As if I were teetering somewhere, waiting to jump, but not knowing where to jump."

"After what happened before," he said, "I am inclined to believe you. Your hunch, that is. Or is it stronger than a hunch?"

"I don't know," she said. "It's so strong that I am frightened—desperately frightened. I wonder—would you spend the night with me? I have a togetherness blanket. Would you share it with me?"

"I'd be pleased and honored."

"Not just because we're a man and woman," she said. "Although I suppose that's a part of it. But because we're two human beings—the only human beings. We need one another."

"Yes," he said, "we do."

"You had a woman. You said the others died . . ."

"Helen," he said. "She's been dead hundreds of years, but to me only yesterday."

"Because you were in sleep?"

"That's right. Time is canceled out by sleep."

"If you wish, you can pretend I'm Helen. I will not mind at all."

He looked at her. "I won't pretend," he said.

25

So there goes your theory, said the scientist to the monk, *about the hand of God brushing across our brows.*

I don't care, said the grande dame. *I don't like this planet. I still think it's ishy. You can get excited about another life-form, another intelligence very much unlike us, but I don't like it any better than I do the planet.*

I must confess, said the monk, *that I do not care too greatly about the idea of bringing even a gallon or so of the Pond aboard. I don't understand why Carter agreed to do it.*

If you recall what passed between Carter and the Pond, said the scientist, *you'll realize that Carter made no promise. Although I rather think we should. If we find a mistake has been made, there is a simple remedy. Anytime we wish, Nicodemus can jettison the Pond, heave it out of the ship.*

But why should we bother with it at all? asked the grande dame. *This thing that Carter calls the god-hour—it is nothing to us. It brushed us, that is all. We sensed it, as Nicodemus did. We did not experience it, as did Carter and Shakespeare. Carnivore—what happened to him we don't really know. He was mostly frightened.*

We have not experienced it, I am sure, said the scientist, *because our minds, which are better trained and disciplined . . .*

Which is only so because we have nothing but our minds, said the monk.

That is true, said the scientist. *As I was saying, with minds better disciplined, we instinctively shunted off the god-hour. We did not let it get to us. But if we opened up our minds to it, we probably would derive much more from it than do any of the others.*

Even if that should not be the case, said the monk, *we'll have Horton on board. He is quite good at it.*

And the girl, said the grande dame. *Elayne—is that her name? It will be good to have two humans back on board again.*

That wouldn't work for long, said the scientist. *Horton or the two of them, whichever it may be, must go into cold-sleep very shortly. We can't allow our human passengers to age. They represent a vital resource we must make the most of.*

But for only a few months? asked the grande dame. *In a few months, they'd be able to pick up a good deal from the god-hour.*

We can't afford a few months, said the scientist. *A human life is short, at best.*

Except for us, said the monk.

We can't be entirely sure how long our lives may be, said the scientist. *At least not yet, we can't. Although I would suggest that, in the full meaning of the term, we may be no longer human.*

Of course we are, said the grande dame. *We are far too human. We cling to our identities and individualities. We quarrel among ourselves. We let our prejudice show through. We still are petty and objec-*

tionable. And we were not meant to be that way. The three minds were supposed to flow together, to become one mind much greater and more efficient than three minds. And I'm talking not only about myself, with my pettiness, which I am quite willing to confess, but you, Sir Scientist, with your exaggerated scientific viewpoint that you tend to flaunt to prove your superiority over a simpleminded, flighty woman and a dumb bunny of a monk . . .

I will not deign to debate with you, said the scientist, *but I must remind you that there have been times . . .*

Yes, times, said the monk. *When deep in interstellar space, there were no distractions, when we had worn ourselves out with our pettiness, when we were bored to death. Then we came together out of sheer weariness and those were the only times when we came close to the fine-honed communal mind that it was expected by those back on Earth we finally would achieve. I'd like to see the look on the faces of all those weighty neurologists and those bird-brained psychologists who worked out the scenario for us if they could only know how all their calculations worked out in actuality. Of course, all of them are dead by now . . .*

It was the emptiness, said the grande dame, *that drove us together. The emptiness and the nothingness. Like three frightened children huddling together against the emptiness. Three minds huddling together for mutual protection and that was all it was.*

Perhaps, said the scientist, *you have come close to the truth of the situation. In your bitterness, close to the truth.*

I am not bitter, said the grande dame. *If I'm remembered at all, I am remembered as a selfless person who gave of herself all her life and who gave more than any human should be ever expected to give. They will think of me as one who gave up her body and the solace of death to advance the cause . . .*

So, said the monk. *once again it comes down to human vanity and to misguided human hopes, although I do not agree with you on that business about the solace of death. But you're right about the emptiness.*

The emptiness, the scientist thought to himself. *Yes, the emptiness. And it was strange that, as a man who should have understood the emptiness, who should have expected it, he had failed to understand, failed to come to terms with it, but had been seized with the same illogical reaction to it as the other two, in the end developing a shameful fear of it. Emptiness, he had known, was only relative. Space was not empty and he had known it wasn't. Although thinly scattered, there was matter there, much of it made up of fairly complex molecules. He had told this to himself time and time again, saying to himself—it is not empty, it is not empty, there is matter there. Yet, he had not been able to convince himself. For there was in the seeming emptiness of space an uncaring and a coldness that drove one in upon one's self, shrinking from the coldness and uncaring. The worst of the emptiness, he thought, was that it made one seem so small and insignificant and that, he told himself, was the thought to fight against, for life, no matter what its smallness, could not be insignificant. Life, on the face of it, was the one thing, the only thing, that had any meaning to the entire universe.*

And yet, said the monk, *there were times, I recall, when we overcame the fright and no longer huddled, when we forgot the ship, when, as a newborn entity, we strode across the emptiness as if it were quite natural, as if we walked a pasture or the garden. It always seemed to me that this time came, that this condition came about only when we reached a point where it seemed we could bear no more, when we had reached and exceeded the feeble capabilities of humanity— when this time came there was an escape valve of some sort, a compensating situation in which we entered upon a new plane of existence . . .*

I remember, too, said the scientist, *and from the memory I can snatch some hope. How confused we seem to be, able to convince ourselves of our hopelessness and then recalling some small fact that can give us hope. It's all so new to us—that's our trouble. Despite the millennia, it's still too new to us. A situation so unique, so alien to our human concepts, that it's a wonder we're not more confused.*

The grande dame said, *You recall that from time to time, on this planet, we have detected another intelligence, a sort of whiff of another intelligence, as if we were hounds sniffing out an ancient trail. And now that we have felt the full force of the Pond-intelligence— reluctant as I am to say it, for I want no more intelligence—the Pond-intelligence does not seem to be the one that we earlier detected. Is it possible there is yet another great intelligence upon this silly planet?*

The creature-in-time, perhaps, suggested the monk. *The intelligence we detected was very faint, extremely subtle. As if it were trying to hide against detection.*

I doubt that would be it, said the scientist. *A thing encased in time, I should judge, would be undetectable. I can think of no more effective insulation than a shield of arrested time. The terrible thing about time is that we know it not at all. Space, matter and energy—these are factors that we can pretend to recognize, or at least theoretically accept their theoretical values. Time is*

184

the complete mystery. We cannot be certain of its actuality. It has no handle we can grasp to examine it.

So there may yet be another intelligence—an unknown intelligence?

I do not care, said the grande dame. *I have no wish to know it. I hope that this pretty puzzle in which we've become involved comes to an early end so we can get out of here.*

It won't be long, said the monk. *A few more hours, perhaps. The planet's closed, and there is nothing further to be done. In the morning, they'll go down and look at the tunnel and then will know there's nothing to be done. But before that happens, there is a decision that must be made. Carter has not asked us because he is afraid to ask us. He fears the answer we will give.*

The answer is no, said the scientist. *Much as we may regret it, the answer must be no. Carter may think harshly of us. He may say we've lost our humanity with our bodies, that we retain only the coldness of our intellect. But that will be his softness speaking, forgetting that we must be hard, that softness has but little part to play out here, away from our own conditioned planet. And, furthermore, it would be no kindness to the Carnivore. He'd drag out his weary life within this metal cage, with Nicodemus hating him and him hating Nicodemus—perhaps afraid of Nicodemus—and that would be heaping coals upon his shame, that he, a warrior of repute who has killed many evil monsters, should be reduced to fearing a spindly mechanism such as Nicodemus.*

With reason, said the monk, *for Nicodemus undoubtedly, in time, would kill him.*

He is so uncouth, said the grande dame, a shudder in

her thought. So lacking in sensibilities, with none of the niceties nor considerations . . .

Which do you mean? asked the monk. *Carnivore or Nicodemus?*

Oh, not Nicodemus. I think he is cute.

26

POND cried out in terror.

Hearing it with the far edges of his mind, Horton stirred in the warmth and nearness, the intimacy and the nakedness, clinging to the closeness of another human—a woman, but with the humanity as important as the woman, for in this place, they were the only humans.

Pond cried out again, a shrill ripple of alarm, slicing through Horton's brain. He sat up in the blanket.

"What is it, Carter Horton?" Elayne asked sleepily.

"It's Pond," he said. "There is something wrong."

The first flush of dawn ran up the eastern sky, shedding a ghostly half-light in which the trees and the Shakespeare house stood out hazily. The fire had burned low, into a bed of coals that winked with blood-red eyes. Beyond the fire Nicodemus stood, facing in the direction of the Pond. He stood stiff and straight, alert.

"Here are your pants," said Elayne. Horton reached out a hand and took them.

"What is it, Nicodemus?" he asked.

"Something screamed," said the robot. "Not so you could hear it. But I could sense the screaming."

Struggling into his trousers, Horton shivered in the dawn chill.

The cry came again, more urgent than it had been before.

"Look what's coming up the path," said Elayne, her voice tight.

Horton turned to see and gulped. There were three of them. They were white and smooth and looked like upended slugs, greasy and repulsive things such as might be found beneath a rock that had been overturned. They came rapidly, hopping on the lower, tapered end of their bodies. They had no feet but that didn't seem to bother them. They had no arms nor faces—they were just fat, happy slugs, skipping rapidly up the path that led down to the tunnel.

"Three more who are marooned," said Nicodemus. "We're getting to be quite a colony. How do you think it happens that so many are coming through that tunnel?"

Carnivore came stumbling through the door of Shakespeare House. He stretched and scratched himself.

"Who the hell are them?" he asked.

"They haven't introduced themselves," said Nicodemus. "They just now showed up."

"Funny-looking, are they not?" said Carnivore. "They haven't got no feet, they just hippety along."

"There is something happening," said Elayne. "Something dreadful. I felt it last night, remember, that something was about to happen and now it's happening."

The three slugs came up the path, paying no attention to those who stood about the fire, brushing past them to take the path that led to the Pond.

The light in the east had brightened, and from far off in the forest something made a sound that sounded like someone dragging a stick along a picket fence.

Another cry from Pond slashed through Horton's mind. He started running down the path that led to the Pond and Carnivore swung in beside him, running with a loping stride.

"Would you disclose to me," he asked, "what has transpired to bring about excitement and so much running?"

"Pond's in some kind of trouble."

"How could Pond be in trouble? Someone throwing rocks at him?"

"I don't know," said Horton, "but he's screaming plenty loud."

The path curved as it crossed the ridge. Below them lay the Pond and beyond the Pond, the conical hill. Something was happening to the hill. It was thrusting up and breaking apart, and out of it was rising something dark and horrible. The three slugs were huddled together, crouching, on the shore.

Carnivore sped up, loping swiftly down the path. Horton yelled at him. "Come back, you fool! Come back, you crazy fool!"

"Horton, look," cried Elayne. "Not at the hill. Up on the city ridge."

One of the buildings, Horton saw, had shattered, its masonry wrenched apart, and out of it was emerging a creature that glittered in the morning sun.

"It's our time creature," said Elayne. "The one we found."

Looking at it in the block of frozen time, Horton had been unable to discern its shape, but now, unfolded from its prison, it seemed a thing of glory.

Great wings were stretching out, and the light flared off them in a rainbow of many colors, as if they were constructed of many tiny prisms. A savage beaked head was poised on a longish neck and the head, Horton thought, looked as if it might wear a helmet set with precious stones. Curved, gleaming talons extended from the heavy claws and the long tail was barbed with sharp and glistening spines.

"A dragon," Elayne said, softly. "Like the dragons out of the old legends of the Earth."

"Perhaps," said Horton. "No one knows what a dragon was, if there was a dragon."

But the dragon, if it was a dragon, was in trouble. Free of the stout stone house in which it had been imprisoned, it beat its way into the air, its huge wings flapping awkwardly to drive it upward. Flapping awkwardly, Horton thought, when it should be skimming into the sky with wings that were strong and sure, climbing the staircase of the air as a fleet-footed being would run joyously up a hill, exulting in the strength of legs, the capacity of lungs.

Remembering Carnivore running down the path, he turned his head to see where he might be. While he did not immediately catch sight of Carnivore, he saw that the hill just beyond the Pond had rapidly broken up, shattered and fragmented by the creature that was clawing its way from it. Great slabs and broken chunks of the hill were rolling down the steepness of its sides and a large amount of debris—stone and soil—had accumulated about its foot. The lower reaches of the hill, still intact, bore cracks that ran in jagged lines, the kind of cracks that an earthquake might open up.

But while he saw all this, it was the emerging creature that claimed his attention.

It dripped with filthiness, great patches of foulness scaling off it. Its head was a blob and the rest of it as well—a great blob that had a semblance of being humanoid, but was not. The kind of horrible travesty of humanity that some barbaric witch doctor, drooling venom, would fashion out of clay and straw and dung to represent an enemy that he sought to torture and destroy—lumpy, misshapen, lopsided, but with an evil in it, a vicious, drooling evil borrowed from the one who made it and magnified by the ineptness of itself. The evil rose from it as a poisonous vapor might rise from a murky swamp.

The hill was almost leveled now, and as Horton watched in fascination, the monster tore itself free and took a stride forward, covering a good twelve feet in that single stride.

Horton's hand drove down, clawing for his gun, realizing even as he did that he did not have the gun—that it was back at camp, that he had forgotten to fasten on his gunbelt, cursing himself for his forgetfulness, for there could be no question, not a shred of doubt, that an evil thing such as the creature that had hatched from out the hill could not be allowed to live.

It was not until this moment that he sighted Carnivore.

"Carnivore!" he shouted.

For the demented fool was running straight toward the creature, running on all fours for better speed. He was charging with his head held low, and even from where he stood, Horton could see the smooth flow of his mighty muscles as he drove himself along.

Then he leaped for the monster and was swarming up its massive body, the momentum of his charge carrying him up the body toward the short length of neck that tied the blob of the head to the lump that was the body.

"NO! NO!" Nicodemus was crying back of him. "Leave it to Carnivore."

Horton swung his head about and saw that Nicodemus had one metal claw wrapped about the wrist of the hand in which Elayne held her gun.

Then he turned his head back swiftly to see Carnivore swing his tiger-head in a slashing, chopping blow. The gleaming tusks sliced into the monster's throat and tore through it. A gush of blackness came out of the throat, spouting, covering Carnivore's body with a dark substance that, for an instant, seemed to blend him with the dark body of the monster. One of the monster's clublike hands reached up, as if in reflex action, and closed on Carnivore, plucking him from its body, lifting him and hurling him away. The monster took another step and began to fall, crashing forward slowly, as a tree might fall to the final ax-stroke, reluctant to fall, striving to stay erect.

Carnivore had fallen on the rocky shore of the Pond and was not rising. Charging down the path, Horton ran to him, brushing past the three slugs still crouched upon the shore.

Carnivore was lying face down and, kneeling beside him, Horton slowly turned him on his back. He was limp and sacklike. His eyes were closed and blood was running from his nostrils and the corner of his mouth. His body was befouled by the sticky black substance that had gushed from the monster's severed throat. Splintered, jagged bone thrust out of his chest.

Nicodemus trotted up and knelt beside Horton. "How is he?" he asked.

"He's alive," said Horton, "but maybe not for long. You don't happen to have a surgeon's transmog in that kit of yours?"

"A simple one," said the robot. "Knowledge of simple illnesses, how to deal with them. Some of the principles of medicine. Nothing that could take care of that rib cage."

"You shouldn't have stopped me," Elayne said to Nicodemus, speaking bitterly. "I could have killed that monster before it laid a hand on Carnivore."

"You don't understand," said Nicodemus. "Carnivore needed it."

"You don't make sense," she said.

"What he means," said Horton, "is that Carnivore's a warrior. He specialized in killing monsters. He went from world to world, seeking out the most deadly species. It was a cultural thing. He got high points for doing it. He was very near the top killer of his people. This one, more than likely, will make him the greatest killer ever. It will give him a sort of cultural immortality."

"But what's the use of it?" she asked. "His people will never know."

"Shakespeare wrote about that very thing," said Nicodemus. "He gained the impression that somehow they would."

One of the slugs, hopping gently, came up and crouched opposite Horton, Carnivore between them. A tentacle extruded from his soft, pulpy body and the tip of it felt carefully over Carnivore's body. Horton looked up, expecting to look into the face of the slug, not remembering that there was no face. The blunt upper end of the body looked back at him—looked back as if there had been eyes. No eyes, and yet the sense of looking. He felt a tingling in his brain, a faint, eerie tingling as if a weak electrical current might be running through it, a sensation that was queasily unpleasant.

"It's trying to talk with us," said Nicodemus. "Do you feel it, too?"

"What is it you want?" asked Horton of the slug. When he spoke, the electric tingling in his brain made a little jump—a jump of recognition?—then went on tingling. Nothing further happened.

"I don't think there's any use," said Nicodemus. "It's trying to tell us something, but there is no way it can. It can't reach us."

"Pond could talk to us," said Horton. "Pond talked with me."

Nicodemus made a shrug of resignation. "These things are different. A different kind of mind, a different kind of signal."

Carnivore's eyes fluttered open.

"He's coming to," said Nicodemus. "He's going to be hurting. I'll go back to camp. I think I have a hypodermic."

"No," said Carnivore, speaking feebly. "No needle in the butt. I hurt. It not for long. The monster, it is dead?"

"Very dead," said Horton.

"Is good," said Carnivore. "I cut its goddamn throat. I be very good at that. I am good at monsters."

"You'll have to take it easy," said Horton. "In a little while, we'll try to move you. Get you back to camp."

Carnivore closed his eyes wearily. "No camp," he said. "Here as good as anywhere."

He coughed, choking on the new blood that splashed out of his mouth and ran across his chest.

"What happened to the dragon?" asked Horton. "Is it anywhere about?"

"It crashed across the Pond," said Elayne. "There was something wrong with it. It couldn't fly. It tried to fly and fell."

"Too long in time," said Nicodemus.

The slug lifted its tentacle and touched Horton's shoulder to gain his attention. It gestured up the shore where the monster lay, a black lump on the land. Then it tapped Carnivore three times and tapped itself three times. It grew another tentacle, and with the two of them made a motion as if to pick up Carnivore and hold him tight against itself, cradling him, holding him with tenderness.

"It's trying to say thank you," Nicodemus said. "Trying to thank Carnivore."

"Maybe trying to tell us it can help him," said Elayne.

His eyes still closed, Carnivore said, "There's nothing that can help me. Just leave me here. Don't move me till I'm dead."

He coughed again.

"And don't, in kindness, tell me I'm not dying. You'll stay with me until it's done?"

"We'll stay with you," said Elayne.

"Horton?"

"Yes, my friend."

"If this hadn't happened, you would have taken me? You'd not have left me here. You would have taken me when you left the planet?"

"We'd have taken you," said Horton.

Carnivore closed his eyes. "I knew you would," he said. "I always knew you would."

By now it was full day, the sun a hand's-breadth above the horizon. The slanting sunlight glittered off the Pond.

And now, thought, Horton, it didn't really matter about the tunnel's being closed. Carnivore no longer would be marooned in this place he hated. Elayne would leave in the Ship, and there would be no need of staying longer. Whatever had been meant to transpire upon this planet was done and ended now. And, he thought, I wish that I could know, perhaps not now, but some day, what it was all about.

"Carter, look!" said Nicodemus in a quiet, tense tone. "The monster . . ."

Horton jerked up his head and looked, gagging at the sight. The monster, lying just a few hundred feet away, was melting. It was falling in upon itself, a putrescent mess. It writhed in seeming life as it sank into a stinking, obscene puddle, with little streams of steaming nastiness flowing from the puddle.

He watched in horrified, offended fascination as it went down to an oily, nauseous scum and the unbidden thought came across his mind that now he could never fix quite straight in mind the shape that it had held. The only impression that he had gained in that moment before Carnivore had slashed the life from it was a lumpiness, a distorted lumpiness that really was no shape at all. That might be the way with evil, he thought—it had no shape at all. It was a lumpiness and a puddled pool of filth and you never knew quite what it was, so that you were left quite free to imagine what it was, driven by the fear of the unknown to clothe it in whatever fashion seemed most horrible to you. So that evil might take on as many guises as there were men to clothe it—each man's evil would be a little different from every other man's.

"Horton."

"Yes, Carnivore, what is it?"

The voice was low and raspy and Horton went on his knees beside him, bending close so that he could hear.

"When it's done," said Carnivore, "you'll leave me here. Leave me in the open where I can be found."

"I don't understand," said Horton. "Found by what?"

"The scavengers. The cleaners-up. The morticians. Little hungry skitterers that will ingest anything at all. Insects, birds, small animals, worms, bacteria. You will do it, Horton?"

"Of course I'll do it if you wish. If that's what you really want."

"A giving back," said Carnivore. "A final giving back. Not begrudging the little hungry things my flesh. Making myself an offering to many other lives. One great final sharing."

"I understand," said Horton.

"A sharing, a giving back," said Carnivore. "Those are important things."

27

As they made their way around the Pond, Elayne said, "The robot is not with us."

"He's back there with Carnivore," said Horton. "He's keeping one last vigil. It's his way of doing things. A sort of Irish wake. But you'd not know of Irish wakes."

"No, I wouldn't. What's an Irish wake?"

"Sitting with the dead. Posting vigil over them. Nicodemus did it with the other humans who were on the ship with me. On a lonely planet of an unknown sun. He wanted to pray for them; he tried to pray and couldn't. He thought it was not proper for a robot to try to say a prayer. So he did something else for them. He stayed awhile with them. He did not hurry off."

"How beautiful of him. It was better than a prayer."

"I think so, too," said Horton. "You're sure you know where the dragon fell? There's still no sign of it."

"I watched it fall," she said. "I think I know the place. It's just over there."

"Remember how we wondered why the dragon was encased in time," said Horton, "if it were encased in time. Writing our own scenario to push back the fact that we knew exactly nothing. Creating our own little human fable to give some meaning and some explanation to an event that was beyond our understanding."

"To me," she said, "it seems quite apparent now why it was left here. It was left here to wait until the monster hatched, to kill the monster when it hatched. By some means, the hatching of the monster would trigger the time trap to turn the dragon loose, and it did turn the dragon loose, for all the good it did."

Horton said, "They—whoever they might be—chained the dragon in time against the day when the monster hatched. They must have known the egg had been laid and if they knew that, why didn't they seek and destroy the egg—if it was an egg—or whatever it might be? Why all the dramatic mumbo-jumbo?"

"Maybe they knew only that the egg had been laid, but had no idea where."

"But the dragon was located less than a mile . . ."

"Maybe they knew the general area. Even so, finding the egg would be like sifting through acres of sandy beach, looking for an object that might have been hard to distinguish even should it be uncovered—so camouflaged that even if you looked directly at it, you might not recognize it. And they might not have had the time to look. They had to leave here for some reason, perhaps rather quickly, so they installed the dragon in the vault and when they left the planet, closed down the tunnel so that if something happened and the dragon failed to kill the monster, the monster couldn't leave the planet.

"And the hatching. We talk about the monster hatching, but I don't think the term is quite correct. Whatever brought the monster into being must have taken a long time. The monster must have undergone a long period of development before it broke from the hill. Like the old seventeen-year locust out of Earth, or at least the old story about the seventeen-year locust. Except that the monster took much longer than seventeen years.''

"What puzzles me,'' said Horton, "is why whoever laid the trap for the monster by putting the dragon into time should have feared the monster so greatly to go to such great pains. The monster was big, sure, and an unlovely thing, but Carnivore ripped his throat out with one stroke, and that was the end of him.''

Elayne shuddered. "He was evil. You could feel the evil pouring out of him. You felt it, didn't you?''

"I felt it,'' Horton said.

"Not just a little evil, as so much of life displays a little evil, or is capable of a little evil. Rather, there was a depth of evil in him that could not be measured. It was an absolute negation of everything that is good and decent. Carnivore caught it by surprise, before it had a chance to bring all its evil into focus. It was new-hatched, barely aware, when he came upon it. That is the only reason, I am sure, that he was able to do what he did.''

By now they had rounded the curve of the Pond below the height of land on which the ruined houses stood.

"I think it's up there,'' said Elayne. "Just up the hill.''

Leading the way, she began to climb. Looking back, Horton saw Nicodemus, reduced to toy proportion by distance, standing on the opposite shore. It was only with some difficulty that he could make out Carnivore's body, which tended to blend in with the barren shelf of rock on which it lay.

Elayne had reached the crest of the hill and halted. When he climbed up beside her, she pointed. "There,'' she said. "There it is.''

A million jewels were sparkling in the underbrush.

The dragon could not be seen because of the intervening vegetation, but the rainbowed reflection of its body showed where it had fallen.

"It's dead," said Elayne. "It's not moving."

"Not necessarily dead," said Horton. "It could be injured, but alive."

Together they went plunging through the brush and when they were past a massive tree with low-hanging branches, they could see the dragon.

It was a thing of breath-catching beauty. Each of the tiny scales that covered the body was a point of gemlike light, little exquisitely colored jewels glinting in the sunlight. When Horton moved forward a step the entire body seemed to flare, the angle of the scales acting as a reflector that threw back the brightness of the day full into his face. But as he made another step, changing the angle of the scales in relation to himself, the flare came to an end and the sparkling came back, as if it were a tinseled Christmas tree entirely covered and obscured by little flashing lights, but lights far more colorful than a Christmas tree could ever wear. Deep blues and ruby reds, greens shading from the paleness of an evening springtime sky to the deep green of an angry sea, living yellow, the sunlit shine of topaz, the pink of apple blossoms, the autumn gleam of pumpkins—and all the colors frosted over with the kind of scintillation that one might see on a frosty winter morning when everything was diamonds.

Elayne drew in her breath. "How beautiful!" she gasped. "More beautiful than we guessed when we saw it in the time vault."

It was smaller than it had seemed when glimpsed flying in the air and it was lying very quietly. One gossamer wing thrust out from the slender body and sagged to lie upon the ground. The other was crumpled underneath it. The long neck was twisted so that the head rested with one cheek upon the ground. Seen close, the head still bore the look of a helmet. On the head the scales that covered the rest of the body were lacking. The helmet was shaped of hard structures that resembled polished metal plates. The massive beak, thrust out from the helmet mask, also had a look of metal.

Still lying quietly, unstirring, the eye in that part of the head that lay uppermost came open—a blue eye, a gentle eye, clear and limpid and unfrightened.

"It's alive!" cried Elayne and started toward it. With a cry of warning, Horton put out a hand to stop her, but ducking past him, she dropped to her knees beside the cruel head, reached out and took it in her arms and lifting it, held it close against her breast.

Horton stood petrified, afraid to move, afraid to make a single sound. A wounded, hurting creature, one thrust, one chop of that wicked beak . . .

But nothing happened. The dragon did not move. Tenderly, Elayne let the head back to the ground, reached out a hand to stroke the jeweled neck. The dragon blinked a long, slow blink, its one eye fastened on her.

"It knows that we are friends," she said. "It knows that we won't hurt it."

The dragon blinked again and this time the eye stayed shut. Elayne went on stroking the creature's neck, crooning quietly to it. Horton stood where he was, listening to the soft crooning, the only sound (scarcely a sound) in a terrible quietness that had settled on the hilltop. Below him and across the Pond the toy that was Nicodemus still stood upon the shore beside

202

the blotch that was Carnivore. Farther up the shore he could make out the larger blotch that was the shattered hill from which the monster had emerged. Of the monster there was no sign at all.

He had known, he thought, about the monster—or he should have known. Only yesterday he had climbed the hill, going on hands and knees because that was the only way one could climb its steepness. Short of the top he had stopped and rested, lying flat upon his belly, and had sensed a vibration in the hill, like the beating of a heart. But he'd told himself, he recalled, that it was no more than his own heart beating, thumping with the exhaustion of the climb, and had thought no more of it.

He looked back at the dragon and sensed the wrongness in it, but it took some time, even so, to know what the wrongness was.

"Elayne," he said, softly. "Elayne."

She looked up at him.

"The dragon's dead," he said. "The color is fading."

As they watched, the fading continued. The tiny scales lost their sparkle and the beauty went away. No longer a thing of wonder, it because a great gray beast and to one watching, there could be no doubt that it had died.

Slowly Elayne got to her feet, wiped her tear-wet face with balled fists.

"But why?" she asked, wildly. "Why? If it were encased in time—if time had been stopped for it—it should have been as fresh and strong as the moment that it was placed in time. Time simply would not have existed for it. There would have been no change."

"We don't know about time," said Horton. "Maybe those who put it into time didn't know as much about it as they thought they did. Perhaps time can't be controlled as easily and as reliably as they thought it could. There still could have been bugs in what they might have considered a perfect technique.''

"You're saying that something went wrong with the time vault. That there could have been a leakage.''

"There is no way that we can know,'' said Horton. "Time is still the great mystery to us. It is no more than a concept; we don't know if it even exists. The vault could have had unsuspected effects on living tissue or on mental processes. Life energy could have been drained away, metabolic poisons could have built up. Perhaps the length of duration was longer than the people who put the dragon into time had calculated. Some factor may have held up the hatching of the monster far beyond the usual length of time such a hatching should have taken.''

"It is strange,'' she said, "how events work out. If Carnivore had not been trapped upon this planet, the monster might be loose.''

"And Pond,'' said Horton. "If Pond had not alerted us, had not let out its shriek of warning . . .''

"So that is what it was. That is how you knew. Why should Pond have been afraid?''

"It probably sensed the evil of the monster. Pond, perhaps, is not immune from evil.''

She came up the little slope and stood close beside Horton. "The beauty of it gone,'' she said. "That's a terrible thing. There is so little beauty in the universe; we can spare none of it. Maybe that's why death is so horrible; it takes away the beauty.''

"The twilight of the gods,'' said Horton.

"The twilight . . .''

"Another old Earth story,'' he said. "The monster,

204

the dragon and Carnivore. All of them dead. A great final reckoning."

She shivered in the warmth of the blazing sun.

"Let's go back," she said.

28

THEY sat about the dying campfire.

"Is there anyone," asked Nicodemus, "who feels like having breakfast?"

Elayne shook her head.

Horton rose slowly to his feet. "It's time to go," he said. "There's nothing more to keep us here. I know that and yet I seem to feel a strange reluctance to leave. We've been here only three days, but it seems much longer. Elayne, you are going with us?"

"Of course," she said. "I thought you knew."

"I suppose I did. Just asking to make sure."

"If you want me and there's room."

"We want you and there's room. There is a lot of room."

"We'll want to take along Shakespeare's book," said Nicodemus. "I guess that's all. On the way back we could stop and pick up a pocket full of emeralds. I know that to us they may be worthless, but I can't get out of the habit of regarding them as valuable."

"There's one other thing," said Horton. "I promised Pond I'd take some of him along. I'll get one of the bigger jugs Shakespeare collected from the city."

Elayne spoke quietly. "Here come the slugs. We'd forgotten all about them."

"They're easy things to forget," said Horton.

"They slither in and out. They're unreal somehow. They're hard to keep in mind, almost as if they intend not to be kept in mind."

"I wish we had the time," said Elayne, "to find out what they are. It couldn't have been just coincidence that they turned up exactly when they did. And they did thank Carnivore, or it looked as if they were thanking him. I have a feeling they played a greater part in all of this than we can ever guess."

The foremost slug had grown a tentacle and was waving it at them.

"Maybe," said Elayne, "they've just found out that the tunnel's closed."

"They want us to go with them," said Nicodemus.

"They probably want to show us that the tunnel's closed," said Horton. "As if we didn't know."

"Even so," said Elayne, "we probably should go with them and find out what they want."

"If we can," said Nicodemus. "The communication is not too good."

Horton led the way, with Elayne and Nicodemus following close behind. The slugs disappeared around the bend that hid the tunnel from view and Horton hurried after them. He rounded the bend and came to a sudden halt.

The tunnel mouth was no longer dark; it gleamed with milky whiteness.

Behind Horton, Nicodemus said, "Poor Carnivore. If he could only be here."

"The slugs," said Elayne. "The slugs . . ."

"The people of the tunnel, could that be it?" asked Horton.

"Not necessarily," said Nicodemus. "The keepers of the tunnels, maybe. The guardians of the tunnels. Not the builders, necessarily."

The three slugs were hopping down the path. They did not stop. They reached the tunnel mouth and hopped into it, disappearing.

"The control panel has been replaced," said Nicodemus. "The slugs must have been the ones who did it. But how could they have known that something was about to happen that would enable them to open the tunnel? Somehow, someone must have known that the hatching was about to occur and that the planet could be opened."

"It was Carnivore who made it possible," said Horton. "He pestered us, he breathed on us, he kept prodding us to get the tunnel open. But, in the end, he was the one who finally got it open, who made it possible. And too late to do him any good. Although we can't feel sorry for him. He got what he wanted. He carried out his purpose and there are few who do. His glory-search is over, and he's a great folk hero."

"But he's dead," said Nicodemus.

"Tell me," said Horton, rmemebering his talk with Shakespeare. "First tell me what is death."

"It's an end," said Nicodemus. "It's like turning out a light."

"I'm not so sure," said Horton. "Once I would have agreed with you, but now I'm not quite sure."

Elayne spoke in a small-girl voice. "Carter," she said. "Carter listen to me, please."

He turned to face her.

"I can't go with you," she said. "It all is changed. It is different now."

"But you said . . ."

"I know, but that was when the tunnel still was closed, when there seemed no chance of it being opened. I want to go with you. There's nothing I want more. But now . . ."

"But now the tunnel's open."

"It's not only that. Not only that I have a job to do and now can continue with that job. It's the slugs. Now I know what I am looking for. I have to find the slugs. Find them, somehow talk with them. They can tell us what we need to know. No more blind probing to learn the secret of the tunnels. Now we know who can tell us what we need to know about them."

"If you can find them. If you can talk with them. If they will talk with you."

"I'll have to try," she said. "I'll leave word along the way, messages at many other tunnels, hoping they will be found by many other searchers, so that if I fail, there'll be others who will know and carry on the hunt."

"Carter," said Nicodemus, "you know she has to do it. Much as we might want her with us, we must recognize . . ."

"Yes, of course," said Horton.

"I know you won't, you can't, but I have to ask," she said. "If you'd come with me—"

"You know I can't," said Horton.

"Yes, I know you can't."

"So it all comes down to this," said Horton. "There's no way we can change it. Our commitments—both our commitments—are too deep. We meet, then go our separate ways. It is almost as if this meeting never happened."

"That's not right," she said, "and you know it isn't. Our lives, each of our lives, have been changed a little. We shall remember one another."

She lifted her face. "Kiss me once," she said. "Kiss me very quickly so there is no time to think, so I can walk away . . ."

29

HORTON knelt beside the Pond and lowered the jug into the liquid. The liquid gurgled as it flowed into the jug. Displaced air made bubbles on the surface.

When the jug was filled he rose and tucked it underneath his arm.

"Good-bye, Pond," he said, feeling silly as he said it, for it was not good-bye. Pond was going with him.

That was one of the advantages to a thing like Pond, he thought. Pond could go many places, yet never leave where it had been to start with. As if, he thought, he could have gone with Elayne and could as well have gone with Ship—and, come to think of it, have stayed on Earth and been dead these many centuries.

"Pond," he asked, "what do you know of death? Do you die? Will you ever die?"

And that was silly, too, he thought, for everything must die. Someday, perhaps, the universe would die when the last flicker of energy had been expended and, when that happened, time would be left alone to brood over the ashes of a phenomenon that might never come again.

Futile, he wondered. Was it all futility?

He shook his head. He could not bring himself to think so.

Perhaps the god-hour had an answer. Perhaps that

great blue planet knew. Someday, perhaps millennia from now, Ship, in the black reaches of some distant sector of the galaxy, would be told or would ferret out the answer. Perhaps somewhere in the context of that answer there might be an explanation of the purpose of life, that feeble lichen which clung, sometimes despairingly, to the tiny flecks of matter floating in an inexplicable immensity that did not know nor care that there was such a thing as life.

30

THE grande dame said, *So now the play is done. The drama is run out and we can leave this cluttered, messy planet for the cleanness that is space.*

The scientist asked, *You've fallen in love with space?*

The kind of thing I am, the grande dame told him, *I cannot fall in love with anything at all. Tell me, Sir Monk, what kind of things we are. You are good at coming up with answers to such foolish questions.*

We are consciousnesses, said the monk. *We are awarenesses. That is all we're supposed to be, but we still are hanging onto assorted garbages that we once had carried with us. Hanging onto them because we think they give us identities. And that is the measure of our selfishnesses and our self-conceits—that conformations such as we still must strive for identities. And the measure of our shortsightedness as well. For there is possible for us a far greater identity—the three of us together—than the little personal identities we continue to insist upon. We can become, if we but allow ourselves, a part of the universe—we can become, perhaps, even as the universe.*

I declare, said the grande dame, *how you do run on. When you get started, there never is any telling to what lengths you'll let yourself be carried. How can you say* we'll become part of the universe? We have, to start with, no idea of what the universe may be, so how can we imagine that we'll become much the same as it?

There is much in what you say, said the scientist, although I do not mean, Sir Monk, any criticism of your thinking when I say this. I have had, in my private moments, some thoughts that are much the same, and the thoughts, I must confess, leave me considerably confused. Man has historically, I believe, looked upon the universe as something that came about through a purely mechanistic evolution that can be explained, at least in part, by the laws of physics and of chemistry. But a universe so evolved, being no more than a mechanistic construct, never would make anything reasonably resembling complete sense since it would not be designed to have any. A mechanistic concept is supposed to make something work, not to make any kind of sense, and it goes against all the logic I can muster to think this is the kind of universe we live in. Certainly the universe is something more than this, although I suppose it is the only way it can be explained by a technological society. I have asked myself in what ways it might be constructed; I have asked myself for what purpose it has been constructed. Surely, I tell myself, not as a simple receptacle to contain matter, space, and time. Certainly it has more significance than this. Was it designed, I ask myself, as the home of intelligent biological creatures and if this is so, what factors have gone into its development to make it such a place, in fact what kind of construct should it be to serve such a purpose? Or was it built simply as an exercise in philosophy?

Or possibly as a symbolism that may not be perceived nor appreciated until that far-distant day when the final distillation of biological evolution has pro-

213

duced some unimaginable intelligence that may finally know the reason and the purpose of the universe? The question is raised, as well, what sort of an intelligence would be required to reach such an understanding. There must, it seems, always be a certain limitation to each evolutionary phase, and there is no way one can be sure that such a limitation would not rule out the capacity to achieve an intelligence necessary to understand the universe.

Perhaps, said the grande dame, *the universe is not meant to be understood. This fetish for understanding may be no more than one mistaken aspect of a technological society.*

Or, said the monk, *of a philosophical society. Perhaps more true of a philosophical society than one that is technological, for technology doesn't give a damn just so the engines run and the equations click together.*

I think you both are wrong, objected the scientist. *Any intelligence must care. An intelligence must necessarily drive itself to the limit of its ability. That is the curse of intelligence. It never lets the creature that possesses it alone; it never lets him rest; it drives him on and on. In the last moment of eternity he will be clinging to the ultimate precipice by his fingernails, kicking and screaming to gather in the final shred of whatever it is that he may be chasing. And he'll be chasing something; I'll lay you odds on that.*

You make it sound so grim, the grande dame said.

At the risk, said the scientist, *of sounding somewhat like a stuffed shirt or a mindless patriot, I might say grim, but glorious.*

None of which points the way for us, said the monk. *Are we going to live out another millennium as three separate, selfish, egotistical identities or are we going*

*to give ourselves a chance to become something else? I
don't know what that something else will be—an equal
of the universe, perhaps the very universe, or something less than that. At the worst, I think, a free mind
divorced from time and matter, able to go anywhere,
perhaps anywhen, we wish without respect to all the
rest of it, rising above the limitations imposed upon our
flesh.*

You are selling us short, said the scientist. *We have
spent only one millennium in our present state. Give us
another millennium, give us ten more millennia. . . .*

But it will cost us something, said the grande dame.
*It will not come for free. What price, Sir Monk, would
you offer for it?*

My fear, said the monk. *I have given up my fear and
I am glad of it. It is no price at all. But it is all I have. It
is all I have to offer.*

And I my bitchy pride, said the grande dame, *and
our Master Scientist his selfishness. Scientist, can you
pay your selfishness?*

It would come hard, said the scientist. *Perhaps
there'll come a time when I'll not need my selfishness.*

Ah, well, said the monk, *we will have the Pond and
the god-hour. Perhaps they'll supply moral support
and maybe some incentive—if no more incentive than
to get the hell away from them.*

I think, said the grande dame, *that we'll finally make
it. Not by getting the hell, as you say, away from
something else. I think that in the end the thing we'll
want to get away from is ourselves. We'll become in
time so sick of our petty selves that each of us will be
glad to merge with the other two. And maybe we can
finally reach that blessed state when we have no selves
at all.*

31

NICODEMUS was waiting by the now-dead campfire when Horton came back from the Pond. The robot had the packs made up and the Shakespeare volume lay on top of them. Horton set the jug down carefully, leaning it against the packs.

''Is there anything else that you want to take?'' asked Nicodemus.

Horton shook his head. ''The book and jug,'' he said. ''I guess that's all. The ceramics that Shakespeare picked up are worthless as they stand. No more than souvenirs. Someday someone else will come along, human or otherwise, who will make a study of the city. Human more than likely. It seems that our species at times may hold an almost fatal fascination for the past.''

''I can carry both the packs,'' said Nicodemus, ''and the book as well. Carrying that jug, you shouldn't be encumbered.''

Horton grinned. ''I have the awful fear that somewhere along the way something will trip me up. I can't let that happen. I have Pond in my custody and can let nothing happen to him.''

Nicodemus squinted at the jug. ''You haven't got much of him there.''

"Enough," said Horton. "A phial of him, a cupful of him probably would be quite enough."

"I don't quite understand," said Nicodemus, "what it is all about."

"Neither do I," said Horton, "except that I have the feeling I'm carrying a jugful of a friend, and out here in this howling wilderness of space a man can ask nothing more."

Nicodemus rose from the woodpile, where he had been sitting. "Pick up the jug," he said, "and I'll shoulder the rest of it. There's nothing more to keep us."

Horton made no move to pick up the jug. He stood where he was, slowly looking around. "I find myself just a bit reluctant," he said. "As if there were something still to do."

"You're missing Elayne," said Nicodemus. "It would have been nice to have her along."

"There's that," said Horton. "Yes, I do miss her. It was hard to stand and watch her walk into the tunnel. And there's him as well." He gestured at the skull that hung above the door.

"We can't take him along," said Nicodemus. "That skull would crumble at the touch. He won't be up there very long. Someday a wind will come along . . ."

"That's not what I mean," said Horton. "He was here alone so long. And now we'll leave him alone again."

"Carnivore's still here," said Nicodemus.

Horton said, relieved, "That's right. I hadn't thought of that."

He stooped and picked up the jug, cradling it carefully in his arms. Nicodemus hoisted the packs to his back and tucked the book underneath an arm. Turning, he started down the path, Horton following.

At the turn of the path Horton turned and looked back at the Grecian house. Getting a good grip on the jug with one hand, he lifted the other arm in a gesture of farewell.

Good-bye, he said, wordlessly, in his mind. Good-bye, you old stormy albatross—you madman, brave man, lost man.

It may have been a trick of shifting light. It may have been something else.

But, in any case, whatever, from his position above the door, Shakespeare winked at him.